*Without thinking, Amy* ~~reached out and gripped~~
*his arm.*

"But don't you see? That's the problem, Charles. He won't talk to me about it." Touching his flesh sent a tingling sensation through her body, and she quickly pulled her hand away. "I just thought perhaps you could speak to him about it—to find out if there's a problem I need to know about. I think he might be more willing to talk to a man about it."

"I'll certainly try, Amy. I see Alex almost every morning when he sells his newspapers along the waterfront. I'll make it a point to talk to the lad tomorrow."

Amy stood and drew her shawl around her shoulders. "I must be going, then. I don't like to trouble you, but if you—"

Charles stood to face her. "I assure you, it's never any trouble to do something to help you, Amy. You're the kindest, loveliest lady I've ever known." He took a step closer to her and held her arms with his big hands. As their eyes locked, time seemed to stand still for both of them, until. . .

**MUNCY G. CHAPMAN** has four children who magically became eight (i.e., their spouses) and then was blessed with eleven grandchildren. All live in Florida. She says she is married to the most wonderful man in the world with whom she recently celebrated their golden wedding anniversary. Muncy likes to sew, cook, play the piano, and, of course, write. She works with the children in her church and also with the shut-ins as a "Caring Caller." She enjoys writing with her husband. He likes the research and she likes choosing the words.

Books by Muncy G. Chapman

## HEARTSONG PRESENTS
HP266—What Love Remembers
HP319—Margaret's Quest
HP361—The Name Game
HP422—Condo Mania

# Red Hills Stranger

*Muncy G. Chapman*

*Heartsong Presents*

*Lovingly dedicated to the two special men in my life,*
*Herb and Lee*

**A note from the Author:**
*I love to hear from my readers! You may correspond with me by writing:*

> Muncy G. Chapman
> Author Relations
> PO Box 719
> Uhrichsville, OH 44683

ISBN 1-58660-866-5

**RED HILLS STRANGER**

Our mission is to publish and distribute inspirational products offering exceptional value and biblical encouragement to the masses.

All Scripture quotations are taken from the King James Version of the Bible.

PRINTED IN THE U.S.A.

## one

America McCutcheon, better known to her friends as Amy, swished her feather duster over the already-pristine leather-bound volumes on the shelf. The many vacancies on the shelves spanning the entire end of Margaret's Millinery and Book Shoppe confirmed that sales had been good during December of 1840. Not a single copy remained of Nathaniel Hawthorne's *Twice-Told Tales,* and just one of Charles Dickens's *Pickwick Papers* was unsold. Amy could only hope that Margaret and Mikal Lee would soon return to the Florida Territory from New York with a fresh supply of books for the customers.

Her supply of hats and bonnets was dwindling too. In spite of the addition of two girls to assist with cutting and basting, orders for holiday bonnets and ball gowns seemed to come in faster than Amy could fill them. Now that Christmas was over, perhaps she would have a few weeks to catch up before the Easter rush began, especially if Margaret would hurry back to help her. Many of their clientele still demanded to have Margaret herself fashion their hats, but Amy's reputation with a needle and thread made her ball-gown creations the envy of Apalachicola society's elite.

Amy's thoughts were interrupted by the clamorous foot-steps of her ten-year-old son as Alex McCutcheon bounced down the stairs with an armload of trash. "Mornin', Mama. Soon as I get this stuff outside to the burn pile, I'll bring in a load of wood for the stove before I go to school. After school, I gotta make a grocery delivery for Mr. Diamanti, but I'll be home before dark. What's for supper tonight?"

Amy shook her head and chuckled. Her young son seemed to have the appetite of two growing boys instead of just one, but she thanked God he was strong and healthy. He was a good lad. Without his help, she wondered how she could manage running the shop during Margaret's long and frequent absences.

When Amy had stumbled into this shop four years ago, practically begging for work, she'd found just a small, one-room millinery shop. But Margaret Porter's kind heart recognized Amy's dire need and made a place for her, even paying little Alex to perform simple chores. Now, four years later, Amy's blessings just seemed to multiply.

The shop had expanded, not only in space but also in merchandise and services. To augment the sales of books and bonnets, Amy used her skill with a needle to turn out gowns for Apalachicola's high-society clientele. She copied designs from *Godey's Lady's Book* and used the elegant fabrics Margaret bought from the textile mills of New York to create gowns that rivaled those worn by the most fashionable women in America. Margaret's little shop had now grown to become the most popular boutique in the western panhandle of the Florida Territory.

Mikal Lee, after his marriage to Margaret Porter in 1838, had built a fine house on Chestnut Street for his new bride; and Amy and her son had been invited to move into the one-room living quarters over the millinery shop where Margaret had lived prior to her marriage.

What a blessing that had proved to be! Now Amy and her son had a safe, comfortable place to live, and her living expenses had been cut almost in half. In addition to the tremendous economic advantage, the convenience was priceless.

Living upstairs over the shop allowed her to work long into the night after Alex was safely asleep on his cot. Mornings she fixed their breakfast over the little cast-iron cookstove and hurried downstairs in time to greet the first customers.

Margaret and Mikal Lee had told her over and over again how happy they were to have a dependable caretaker living on the premises, especially one who could keep their business running smoothly in their absence. *But shouldn't they be back by now?* Amy wondered. It had been well over a month since the Lees had sailed away on the *Windsong* to transport a full load of cotton around the tip of Florida and up the eastern seaboard for delivery to the New York textile mills.

Amy realized how much the cotton growers from Georgia and Alabama depended on Mikal, but didn't he understand that she depended on him too? If he and Margaret didn't get home pretty soon with a load of supplies, she might have to close the shop. Her feather duster gained momentum as Amy struggled to vent some of her frustrations.

At the tinkling sound of the little bell on the door, Amy stashed her duster behind some books and tried to mask her concerns with a smile. A customer always deserved a cheerful welcome, no matter what the problems of the day. "Good morning," she said, turning her attention to the customer. *But wait!* This man coming toward her didn't look like a customer at all.

Tall and brawny, he was badly in need of a haircut and shave. He wore a faded orange shirt of coarsest homespun, his sleeves fringed with tatters and tears. His blue homespun britches, though clean, had large holes in both knees. Surely this man was not here to buy a book. What then was his intent?

Alone in the store, Amy felt a moment of panic, but good manners forced her to ask, "May I help you?"

The stranger held himself proud and erect and met her gaze head-on. "My name is Charles Drake. I'm sorry to interrupt your work, but—"

"Charles Drake." Amy repeated the name and tried to subdue the slight tremor in her voice. "I don't believe I've seen you around here before. Where are you from, Mr. Drake?"

The man shuffled his feet and glanced uneasily toward the door. "I, um, come from the red hills, Ma'am."

*The red hills?* Amy's apprehension mounted. She'd heard tales about the red hills. Forty or so miles to the north, they extended from the Apalachicola River all the way to Tallahassee and were reportedly a haven for outlaws and scalawags.

Charles Drake must have seen the fear in her eyes. "I mean to cause you no trouble, Ma'am, but I wondered if you might have some chores I could do. I'm very strong, and I'd be willing to do whatever you ask."

Amy had begun to shake her head, but then she heard his next sentence. "You wouldn't even have to pay me if you could just give me a bite to eat."

Something about the way he looked at her with sad, blue eyes touched Amy's heart. It was wrong to judge the man merely because of the area from which he came. She thought of the story of the Good Samaritan. *Is this stranger, then, my neighbor?*

His speech and his manners were that of an educated man—albeit a man down on his luck. She remembered what it felt like to be hungry. Not a good feeling at all.

*"I was a stranger and ye took Me in."* The Lord seemed to be speaking to her as clearly as though He stood beside her.

She recalled the day she had first come into this shop, hungry and looking for work, and had found a woman with a kind and generous heart. Where would she be today if Margaret had turned her away? As a young widow with a child to raise, Amy had had no idea where to turn for help. "Sir, I am not the proprietress of this establishment, but if you wait a moment, I will find something for you to eat."

Relief spread over his face like sunlight creeping from

behind a cloud. He pushed a lock of sandy hair from his forehead. "I'm much obliged to you, Ma'am. I'm not a beggar. I'd prefer if you'd let me do something to earn my meal."

"It's hard to work on an empty stomach." Amy spoke from experience. "I'll get you some food, and then we can talk about work." She was on her way up the steps before he had a chance to answer.

The half pan of corn bread left from last night's supper would have been enough for another meal for Amy and Alex; but she had plenty of cornmeal to make more, so she put the whole of it on a tin plate. She covered the crumbly square of corn bread with a heaping serving of pinto beans ladled from the pot simmering on her cookstove. Thankfully she had soaked the beans overnight and started cooking them early this morning. This was not fancy fare, but it was the kind of food that would stick to a man's ribs.

She hurried down the stairs with her offering, only then remembering that she had left the store unattended. Even Alex had gone. But what was there to steal? Surely this man would rather have food than books or bonnets. Besides, he didn't impress her as a thief. If she had to guess, she would say he was a real gentleman who had known better times. Asking for food must be very degrading for him.

She was surprised to find the room downstairs empty except for two stylishly dressed ladies fingering a clip of swatches on the counter. "Oh, there you are," one of them said. "We wondered if you were closed today or just, um, taking a necessary, um, recess." She colored slightly, then eyed the plate in Amy's hands. "Oh, I see we've interrupted your dinner."

Amy put the plate on the end of the counter. "No, I. . .please, what can I show you today?" She cast her glance around the room, wondering what had happened to her male visitor. She didn't see him anywhere, and she wondered why she felt such a sudden sense of loss and disappointment.

"Is Margaret here?" the second lady asked. "I wanted to talk to her about a hat to wear to the racetrack next month. My husband just insists that I accompany him, though I can't see the attraction of watching a bunch of horses running around in a circle."

"But it's such fun to go there and see what all the other ladies are wearing," her companion chirped. "Who cares what the silly horses are doing?"

Amy tried to suppress the giggle she felt welling up inside her throat. "No, Mr. and Mrs. Lee haven't returned yet from their trip to New York, but I'm expecting them any day. I'm sure she'll come back with lots of new fashion ideas and all the necessary fabrics and notions to create them for her Apalachicola patrons." She opened her notebook and picked up a stub of a pencil. "If you'd like to tell me the colors and the material you have in mind, I'll be sure to discuss them with Margaret as soon as she returns."

The two women exchanged glances and whispered a few words to each other. Then, with a slight shake of her head, the one who had expressed an interest in a new hat said, "No, there's no rush. I'll just come back in when Margaret is here." She hastily amended her remark. "Oh, that's not a reflection on *your* work, my dear. It's just that Margaret has been making hats for me ever since she opened this shop four years ago. But when it's a new gown I'm needing, I'll be sure to come back to talk to *you.*"

Amy smiled. Everyone in town knew she and Margaret each had their own special areas of expertise, and no offense was taken. "Please do, Mrs. Crowder. It's always a pleasure to serve you."

As soon as the store was empty of customers, Charles Drake came through the doorway again. "I'm sorry, Ma'am. I hope I didn't offend your customers. I stepped outside as soon as they came in." He hung close to the door, casting furtive glances outside to make sure the entry was clear of more potential shoppers.

Amy looked at the food on the counter. Surely the beans had grown cold by now. She lifted the plate and held it out to him. "I'm sorry this is no longer hot, but at least it should be filling."

He eyed the plate hungrily but used some mannerly restraint in taking it from her. "I'm much obliged, Ma'am." Stepping forward, he used two hands to accept her offering. "I'll just take this out back and get out of your way to eat it; and when I come back to return your plate, maybe you'll have figured out something for me to do to repay your kindness."

Not having a ready reply, Amy nodded and watched him back his way to the door. Turning, he stepped over the threshold and disappeared from sight.

When he returned with her plate, she'd let him chop some firewood for her stove and carry it up the stairs. Alex would be glad to be relieved of that chore for a day, and it might help assuage Charles Drake's pride.

She couldn't help but wonder what unfortunate experience had reduced this poor man to such dire economic straits and what strange combination of events had led him from the infamous red hills to her door.

❧

Margaret and Mikal Lee stood on the deck of the *Windsong* as the sturdy schooner plowed its way through the choppy waters of the Gulf of Mexico. To the west, the golden sun slid closer to the horizon, blending the medley of the sky's colors into a vibrant painter's palette.

"Do you think we purchased everything we'll be needing for the shop?" he asked.

Margaret's smile spread across her face. "Amy is going to be so excited when she sees the gorgeous fabrics and trims I found. I've never seen such a lovely assortment of ribbons.

Even the buttons were spectacular this season. I'm afraid I let my appetite run away with me. And then to top it all, that unbelievable purchase we made on our last day in New York. The bill must have been enormous."

It was Mikal's turn to smile. He gave his wife an indulgent wink. "It's all paid for, so there's nothing for you to worry your pretty little head about. The price for cotton was higher than I've ever seen it. I have a feeling 1841 is going to be a good year for us all. You just concentrate on turning out your famous hats and bonnets, and let me worry about the bills."

Four-foot waves slapped against the side of the schooner, tossing it from side to side, but the couple lingered on the deck, holding onto the rail for balance. Margaret loved the feel of the salt spray on her face and the wind in her hair. It was on this very spot—the deck of the *Windsong*—that she had first encountered the handsome seaman who was later to capture her heart. He hadn't told her then that he owned the ship!

She, a spoiled young debutante from Savannah, had begun the journey against her father's wishes, without an inkling of how impractical her trunk full of fancy gowns would be in the wild and lawless Florida Territory. Had it not been for the help of Mikal Lee, how would she ever have managed on her own? He became her trusted friend long before she realized how much she loved him.

"Look, Margaret!" Mikal, with his arm around her waist, pulled his wife closer and pointed. "That beam you see sweeping over the water is coming from the lighthouse on Saint George Island. We're almost home."

Margaret's long brown hair blew in a tangled mass across her face, but she pushed it back to get a better view. "Yes. Oh, yes. I can hardly wait to get home." The word "home" excited her as it never had before she and Mikal had moved into their house on Chestnut Street.

"Too bad we can't go across the bay tonight; but it will be

dark before we land at Saint George Island, and I doubt we'll find transportation to the mainland before daybreak."

Margaret stuck out her lower lip in a pout. She knew that large schooners like the *Windsong* couldn't navigate the shallow waters of Apalachicola Bay, and travelers had to depend on smaller crafts and barges to transport them and their goods from Saint George Island to the mainland. But patience was not one of Margaret's virtues—never had been.

"Don't worry, Honey," Mikal said. "We'll just batten down the hatches so the mosquitoes won't carry us away, then spend one more night on the *Windsong*. I'll make you a cup of hot chocolate to help you sleep well; and when you wake up in the morning, we'll find someone to take us across the bay."

They had been married now for more than two wonderful years, yet Mikal still treated her like a new bride. And Mikal was right; 1841 *was* going to be a good year for them. This last trip to New York had been especially amazing, but Margaret was waiting until they reached their own home to share her exciting new secret with her husband.

# two

Amy wadded a scrap of fabric into a tight little ball and pressed it against the pad of the index finger on her right hand. She had been working on Mrs. Winslow's ball gown for the better part of the morning; and even though she always sewed with a thimble, her fingertips ached from pushing the needle through the tough satin material. The aching she could tolerate, but not the spot of blood that had finally worked its way through to the surface of her tender skin. Just one tiny bloodstain could ruin the gown she'd been working on for days, and she could scarce afford such a loss. Better to wait a few minutes just to be sure.

Amy stood up and pressed the palms of her hands against her lower back. Walking to the window, she saw that the sun had risen almost midway in the sky. Alex should have been home by now. It had been hours since he left to sell his morning newspapers; and for the hundredth time, Amy wondered if she had been unwise to let her young son take on such a big responsibility.

Amy never had to coax the boy to rise before first light to go out and sell his papers. Some days he returned home hoarse from the strain of calling, "Extra, extra! Read all about it!" Then he'd have to rush to get across town to his lessons in the little one-room schoolhouse, but he never complained. He was immensely proud of the coins he accumulated from his early morning sales, and he carefully stashed them away in a jar beneath his cot.

Her thoughts were interrupted by the sound of rapid

footsteps across the porch, followed by a gust of wind as the front door flew open.

"They're coming!" Alex ran into the millinery shop to shout the announcement, and Amy didn't need to ask whom he was talking about. His excitement could only mean one thing: Margaret and Mikal were back. *Praise the Lord!*

She felt a tumultuous surge of joy. Except for Alex, those two people were the closest thing she had to a family, and they'd been gone for almost two months. *Oh, my!* How she longed to see them again.

"I heard the men talking about it when I went down to the docks this morning," Alex told her, still breathless from running. "The *Windsong* sailed into the landing on Saint George Island last night, and Cap'n Bud's done gone across the bay to get 'em and bring 'em home. I reckon they oughta be coming in most any minute now. I'm going back down to the waterfront, but I ran home to tell you so's you'd know."

Amy was beside herself with excitement. "Thank you, Son." She wasn't sure she favored having Alex hang around the waterfront so much, but she knew the dockhands liked him and often hired him to run small errands. "You'd better go upstairs and get something to eat before you leave. And Alex, please be careful. I don't know what I'd do without my man of the house." She ruffled his hair affectionately before he squirmed away from her grasp and bounded up the stairs.

*I'd better put a kettle of water on for tea,* she decided. *They'll likely be needing something after that long journey.* She climbed the stairs and dipped enough water from her pail to fill the kettle before placing it on the small cookstove in the corner. She wished she had time to make an apple pie, but she needed to get back downstairs to work on Mrs. Winslow's ball gown. She had promised to have it finished before next weekend.

❧

At midafternoon, the Lees finally arrived at the little

millinery shop on Market Street. Mikal stood aside while Amy and Margaret embraced, and Alex danced around them yelling, "I told you they was back! Didn't I tell you they was back?"

Amy was so happy to see her friends that for once she didn't bother to correct her son's grammar. "Yes, Alex. You told me. Oh, I'm so glad to see you both!" She grabbed Margaret again and gave her an extra squeeze.

Mikal was intently perusing the bookshelves. "Looks like you sold a lot of books over Christmas, Amy. You wouldn't be wanting more, would you?"

Amy's heart skipped a beat. Not wanting more? Was he going to tell her he hadn't brought any books back with him from New York? But when she saw the familiar twinkle in his eye, she realized he was only trying to tease her. "Oh, Mikal! Get on with you. I hope you brought more *Twice-Told Tales*. We don't have a single copy left, and some of our customers were disappointed when they couldn't purchase them for Christmas gifts."

He gave her a playful wink. "We might just find one or two of those in our crates. And speaking of crates, that fellow ought to be getting here with them soon." He went to the door and looked down the street.

"You don't have them with you?" Amy asked. "Who's bringing them?"

"We couldn't wait to get here and see you," Margaret said. "We hired a carriage and came on ahead. But Mikal rented a wagon and horses and hired someone to load our things and bring them to the store. He should be here soon because Mikal stayed around to help him load the biggest pieces. Most everything we brought is for the shop, and the few things we need delivered to our house, we'll pick up later." She untied the knot in her shawl and lifted it from her shoulders. "Oh, Amy, I've so much to tell you. And just wait 'til you see the things we brought back. You're going to love it all, but one thing in particular."

Amy clapped her hands in anticipation. "What is it, Margaret?"

Margaret shook her head and laughed. "I'm not telling. You just have to wait and see."

The sound of wagon wheels and the *clip-clop* of horses' hooves turned their attention to the street. "That must be the fellow I hired," Mikal said, then walked out on the porch to meet him. "Hello there. I see you found us. Here, let me give you a hand unloading those crates. Some of them are pretty heavy."

A fashionably dressed lady entered the store, and Amy ushered her to the back counter. "Good afternoon, Madam. Let's step back here out of the way where we can talk. What may I show you today?"

Amy and her customer were so busy studying designs in the fashion book and comparing fabric swatches to the pictures, they paid scant attention to all the activity at the front of the store. When at last the lady had placed her order and made an appointment to have her measurements taken, Amy walked with her to the front door.

Mikal and his helper were struggling with a large, heavy crate. "That's the one I want opened first," Margaret ordered. "That's the one I can't wait for Amy to see. She is going to be so surprised."

But Amy's big surprise came before the lid was lifted because there, prying the top boards loose, was none other than Charles Drake. Amy blinked her eyes to make sure they weren't playing tricks on her. "Mr. Drake?"

"What? You two know each other?" Now it was Mikal's turn to be surprised.

Charles began to give a straightforward answer. "Yes, the other day when I first got—"

"Yes, we've met," Amy interrupted quickly, hoping to save the poor man the embarrassment of admitting how he had been forced to accept a handout. "How are you, Mr. Drake?" Her cheeks burned, and her heart was hammering in a way she didn't understand. She supposed there was just too much excitement in such a short period of time. "Go ahead and open the box. I'm eager to see what's inside."

Charles pulled back the boards, and Mikal reached through the packing excelsior to extract the strangest piece of equipment Amy had ever seen. Margaret pulled at the pieces of straw clinging to the contraption and asked, "What do you think of that?"

Amy's brow wrinkled as she circled the strange object to examine it from every direction. "What is it?"

"It's a sewing machine," Margaret announced proudly. "As soon as Mikal gets it set up, I'll try to show you how it works."

"A sewing machine? Why, I never heard of such." Amy was clearly skeptical, but Mikal quickly assured her.

"We saw the thing work. It takes a spool of thread and works it into the prettiest little chain stitch you ever did see. Strong too, unless you pull the thread from one end. Then it comes apart just like a crocheted doily."

"Some of the larger garment factories in New York are giving them a try. I predict they'll be quite in demand if they eventually become available for home use, although, of course, they're very expensive."

"Well, I never," Amy repeated over and over again. "I don't think I'd want to trust that kind of seam on one of my gowns. Why, just suppose someone should accidentally pull on the thread and the whole thing fell apart right in the middle of polite company."

Alex shrieked with laughter. "Wouldn't that be a sight?"

Mikal's shoulders shook as at first he tried to contain himself before giving in and joining Alex in the fun. "It purely would,

Alex. But on the bright side, your ma would be famous."

Seeing Amy's crestfallen face, Margaret tried to reassure her. "I'm sure you won't want to use it for everything. At least, not at first. But when you see it sew, you'll agree it's the most amazing invention of the century."

"Next to those strange contraptions John Gorrie keeps working on to cool his patients," Mikal amended. "That's got to be at the top of the list. By the way, how is my friend, Amy? Have you seen John lately?"

Amy was still studying this thing called a sewing machine, but she paused to answer him. "No, but I was glad to hear he and Caroline have moved back to town. Apalachicola really needs a good doctor, what with the recent outbreak of malaria and all."

"From what we heard when we stopped in the port of Tampa on the way home, malaria isn't the worst of it," Margaret said. "They warned us not to stop at Saint Joseph because they've reported several cases of yellow fever in that area. Mikal was glad to be able to tell them we didn't have to go quite that far."

"That's terrible," Amy said. "What a change that must be from last year when all that concerned them was the Constitutional Convention and housing all those delegates who came trying to help Florida achieve statehood."

While the ladies chatted, Mikal and Charles and Alex moved the new sewing machine against the wall and continued to open the sturdy crates, saving each nail in a neat pile to be reused later and stacking the lumber in a pile just outside the front door. The sewing machine had been forgotten for the moment as more and more of the treasures of New York merchants were unveiled.

First came the books. As the men unpacked them, the women wiped the covers with muslin cloths and stacked them on the shelves. "Oh, look," Amy exclaimed. "Here's the latest volume of William McGuffey's *Eclectic Readers*. Alex has already gone through the first three, and I've been hoping we could get the fourth for Miss Slade, the new schoolmarm. I'm sure I'm not the only mother in town who'll be glad to see these."

Alex snorted. "I already know how to read pretty good, Mama. I don't see why you want me to waste my time on things like that."

Charles had spoken little since he arrived, but now he offered a piece of advice to the young boy. "Learn all you can while you're young, Son. In the Good Book, it says 'study to show thyself approved unto God.' Think about that, and be thankful you have someone willing to teach you."

The room grew as quiet as a cemetery, and all eyes turned toward Charles. Who was this man who seemed to have popped up out of nowhere? Amy had the strong feeling that he was far from an ordinary man—that he was someone special. She'd like to know his story, but of course she would never ask. The fact that he quoted from the Good Book was an encouraging sign, but even that was not an absolute guarantee of his character.

One thing that puzzled her was that he wore the same ragged clothes he had worn the day before, but they did not appear to be dirty. She wondered how he managed to keep himself clean. Most people who roamed the dusty roads of Florida had a distinct, unpleasant odor about them; but she detected nothing unpleasant about Charles Drake. Nothing at all. In fact, with a shave and a haircut and some decent clothes, she was certain he would be quite handsome.

"Look at this, Amy," Margaret said, breaking the awkward silence. She pulled a magazine from the box. "It's the latest issue of *Ladies' Companion*. I looked through it on the way home, so I'll leave it here for you to read." Margaret flipped through a few of the pages. "It's chock full of household hints, and it even has a few articles about modern fashions."

Fashions. Yes, that's what she should have her mind on. Not on the strange man who had wandered in from the street looking for food. What was the matter with her? "I'm trying to finish a satin gown for Mrs. Winslow," Amy said, trying to properly prioritize her thoughts. "Perhaps I'll get a new idea from the magazine for a unique embellishment that would make it especially lovely."

The sun had set, and daylight was fast slipping away. Amy brought out her tallow candles, lit them, and placed them about the room, careful to keep them well away from the fabrics and packing materials.

"This box is filled with piece goods," Margaret said. "Just run your hands over this velvet." She pulled out a folded length of fabric for Amy's approval. "And this other box has laces and ribbons and all sorts of fancy trims. There were so many to choose from. I can't wait to begin using some of these on my hats and bonnets."

Luckily business hours were over for the day, because the shop was a mess. The floor was strewn with excelsior and crumpled newspapers, and the men had tracked in clumps of dirt and grime. Amy would have to clean everything thoroughly before she opened for business on the morrow. It would likely be several days before she found a place for everything.

All the boxes had now been opened and pushed to the back wall so that at least the passageways were clear. Alex had worked right alongside the men. Amy wondered if he might be pushing himself a little too hard trying to keep up with them. Even though he was a strong and healthy lad, he was, after all, only ten years old; and he did look a little pale and tired.

"I don't know about the rest of you," Mikal said, "but I'm starved. What say we all go down to the boardwalk and find us some fresh oysters on the halfshell?"

Charles edged toward the door. "I'd best be going, Sir. Do you think you'll be needing my services again tomorrow? It's a real pleasure working for you."

"Tomorrow and the day after too, I think. Charles, I've had trouble finding good help. If you aren't already committed to someone else, I'd like to talk to you about staying on and working with me down at the warehouse."

A look of hope illuminated Charles's face. "Yes, Sir. I'd be pleased to talk to you about that." He continued to back toward the door. "Well, I'll just be moseying on then and let you folks get your supper, but I'll be down at the waterfront at sunup tomorrow. And I thank you kindly, Sir."

Mikal had to grab his arm to keep him from disappearing into the night. "Hold on there, Fella. I know you must be hungry after all that work. What's the matter? Don't you like oysters?"

"Yes, I do, but. . .um, I reckon I'd better not."

"This treat is on me. We're *all* going out to celebrate our homecoming by having a fine feast. You too, Alex. Put on your coat. I haven't had this kind of food since Margaret and I set sail in the fall. New York has some fancy eateries, but nobody in the world has oysters like we have right here in Apalachicola."

# three

Late into the night, after Amy had put all the new merchandise onto shelves and straightened the millinery shop, she trudged wearily up the stairs to bed. She unbraided her hair and brushed it fifty strokes. Kneeling on the cold wooden floor beside her bed, she began her nightly devotion by giving thanks for the safe return of Mikal and Margaret Lee. Her dark, waist-length hair, crimped by the braids she wore by day, fell forward over her face as she bowed in prayer. She always asked the Lord's blessing on Alex. Tonight she also prayed for Charles Drake. She didn't know what kind of troubles he had seen; but God knew, and He would know how to help him.

The room was bathed in moonlight. She lay beneath her quilt and thought back over the amazing experiences of the day.

Alex's soft, steady breathing and the rhythmic rise and fall of his covers assured her he was sleeping soundly. Outside, a barn owl hooted his lonely call, and seconds later Amy heard his mate's reply float gently through the still night air.

Amy knew what it meant to be lonely. Her teenage marriage eleven years ago had been arranged by her father, and she scarcely remembered the husband who had died of influenza before their child was born. But all the pent-up anger she'd felt at her father for pushing her into a loveless marriage dissolved the moment she held her son in her arms. She thanked God every day for giving him to her. Alex was all she had in the world.

Amy's mother had died in childbirth, leaving her to be raised by a father who seemed to care more about gambling and drinking than he did his daughter. As soon as Amy reached marriageable age, he seemed all too eager to push her out the door and relieve himself of the responsibility. She did not even know his whereabouts.

Until now, she had never given a thought to romance. Although she was not yet thirty years old, she always thought of herself as a mature matron, past the age of all that silliness, a widow whose only purpose in life was to raise an honest, God-fearing son. Romance was for the young and foolish. Why then did the image of Charles Drake keep creeping into her mind, causing her heart to pound like a hammer? She didn't know a thing about the man! He was a complete stranger. Was she drifting into a second childhood, dreaming silly and impossible dreams?

Thanks to Mikal's generosity today, they had all been treated to a grand evening, eating smoked oysters under the stars while they listened to country bands pull lively music from their banjos and guitars and harmonicas.

Amy continued to be impressed by the speech and manners of Charles Drake, and she wondered anew how a man of such obvious breeding and education could have been reduced to living like a pauper. Though he didn't have a lot to say tonight, when he did speak, his voice was as soft and as gentle as an ocean breeze. Remembering the sound of it, Amy could only describe it as hypnotic. He was nothing like the throngs of men who frequented the waterfront. Who was Charles Drake, and why was he here?

When the group had strolled along the water's edge, listening to the gulf lap at the sandy shore and watching the beams of the lighthouse play across its choppy surface, Amy had felt enveloped in peace and contentment. And now, hours later, she lay on her bed wondering what had happened this night to change her.

❧

At first light, Amy went downstairs to look over the new stock that lined her shelves. No, it hadn't been a dream.

Rich satins and velvets in deep vivid colors and pastel dimities and silks for summer wear—they were all there. Margaret had thought of everything. Boxes of lace, ribbons, feathers, and every conceivable trim made Amy want to open the newest edition of *Godey's Lady's Book* and begin at once to create something from its pages.

Alex too was up and about early, and he was out the door before she could remind him to button his jacket against the January wind. He liked to be the first boy on the waterfront with the early edition of the morning paper; and if she didn't catch him, he'd often leave without eating his breakfast. Today was such a morning. He'd come back in an hour or two, ravenous and ready to eat everything in sight.

Word of the new shipment of goods must have traveled quickly, because by nine o'clock, the shop was filled with excited ladies, all wanting to see pictures of the latest New York styles. A sprinkling of men came too, wanting to peruse the bookshelves and see what had been added. "Look at this!" one man exclaimed. "*Two Years Before the Mast*, by Richard Henry Dana. I've heard about that. I don't care what anyone says. Apalachicola is certainly not behind the times when it comes to good books."

"Hey, let me see that. Is there more than one copy?"

"What's this contraption over here?" a smartly dressed lady asked, running her hands over the new chain-stitch machine.

"I think it's called a sewing machine," Amy told her. "I can't show you how it works because I don't yet know myself. When Margaret comes in, perhaps she'll show us."

"What will they think of next? A machine that does our sewing for us. Next thing you know, they'll be coming up with machines that wash our clothes and our dishes."

Her remarks brought forth hoots of laughter. "Not likely," one lady commented. "But isn't it great to live in such modern times?"

"I suppose so, but I wouldn't want my gowns messed up with a silly gadget like that. I'll stick with an ordinary needle and thread, thank you."

Amy listened to their chatter while she tried to wait on her customers. She hoped Margaret would come in today to help. Ladies were lined up to pay for their purchases, while others clustered around the fashion books, trying to be the first to commission a creation of some new design. When one of the cutters she had hired walked through the door, Amy put her right to work waiting on customers. She could only hope the girl knew how to properly manage cash.

At last the Lees walked into the shop, and Amy noticed that Mikal was wearing a grin that spread from one ear to the other. If she wondered why he seemed so elated, she didn't have to wait long to find out.

He stepped between two gentlemen who were busy browsing the bookshelves, put his hands on their shoulders, and said in a loud whisper that carried through the room, "Fellows, my wife just told me last night that I'm going to be a *father*! Imagine that! Me, a *father*!" He made it sound as though he was the first man on earth to lay claim to such a title.

The room erupted into decorous giggles and elbow-punching, while Margaret moved back to the farthest corner of the shop to hide her embarrassment. Amy followed her and gave her a hug. "What wonderful news, Margaret. Don't be embarrassed by Mikal's exuberance. I know you've both been hoping this would happen. I'm so happy for you."

"Look at all these people," Margaret exclaimed. "They all heard him." Reluctantly, she moved out of the corner to face the crowd. "I'm mortified. But they all need to be served, so we'd better get to work." She pushed up her sleeves and moved toward the counter to help.

Meanwhile, Mikal took over the sale of books; but Amy could hear his voice over the babble of the crowd, telling the gentlemen who crowded around him, "We'll probably name him Mikal, and I'm going to teach him all about the schooner as soon as he's old enough to handle it. Of course, Margaret will teach him how to read and write and cipher, but I'll make a real man out of him." He wrapped books in paper and made change for his customers; but between each sale, Amy could hear him say, "A father! Imagine that."

Amy wondered if it had crossed his mind that babies came in two varieties, but this did not seem like the best day to remind him. She smiled at his enthusiasm and turned to wait on the next customer.

When at last the crowd thinned and the room became quieter, Amy finally had a chance to talk to Margaret. "About last night, I wanted to thank you and Mikal again for giving Alex and me such a lovely evening. It was so much fun, and the food was delicious. Alex and I don't get to dine out very often, so that was a real treat for both of us."

"It was good, wasn't it? We enjoyed it too. And what did you think of that new man, Charles Drake?"

*Margaret has a way of getting right to the heart of a matter, doesn't she?* Amy hoped she didn't notice the flush she felt rising to her cheeks. "He, um, seemed very nice. But of course I don't really know anything about him." Then after a brief pause, she tried to sound casual when she asked, "Do you?"

Margaret flicked a piece of fabric lint from her arm. "No, only what Mikal told me. The poor man seems to be destitute; but I get the impression he's used to better things, don't you?"

Amy grabbed a cloth and began to vigorously polish the counter. "Yes. Well, I thought maybe he might have told Mikal something about the circumstances that led him to Apalachicola."

Margaret laughed. "Amy, you're going to rub a hole in that counter. No, he didn't. I think Mikal asked him, but he said Charles seemed reluctant to talk about himself. Anyway, you know Mikal and his kind heart. You heard him offer the man a job last night. Well, Mikal said he was there at the warehouse before daybreak, waiting to be put to work. And listen to this. It is so typical of Mikal. He took him a pair of his trousers and two good work shirts. He told Charles he was giving them away because they had gotten too tight for him."

Amy dropped her polishing cloth on the counter. "Oh, Margaret, surely that didn't work. Charles must have known he couldn't fit into something that was too tight for Mikal. Aren't they about the same size?"

"Of course they are. But Mikal couldn't just give the clothes to him as if he were a charity case. That would have hurt the man's pride."

Amy nodded, grasping the full meaning of what Margaret had just said. "You're right. As you put it, that was so typical of Mikal. He is the kindest, most generous man I know. He truly lives his faith. Your baby is going to be richly blessed to have two Christian parents who love him." Amy blinked back a threatening tear. "I try to be both mother and father to Alex, but it's very hard to raise a son without a man in the house."

Margaret put an arm around her shoulder. "I'm sure it's hard, Amy, but you're doing a wonderful job with Alex. Why, anyone would be proud to have a son like him."

"Thank you, Dear. Anyway, I'm glad Mikal gave Charles a change of clothes. I kept wondering how he kept himself clean. He didn't seem to have the smell of a drifter. He must have used the salty water from the Gulf of Mexico to wash himself and his clothes."

"I suppose so. Anyway, he seemed so anxious to work and so grateful for the job that Mikal told him he could live in that back room of the warehouse. There's a lot of riffraff roaming the waterfront at night, and Mikal is glad to have someone on hand to keep an eye on things." She sighed and wrinkled her brow. "I asked Mikal how he could put so much trust in a man he had only just met, but he told me he has a feeling for that sort of thing. I think it had something to do with the way the man looked him square in the eye when he talked. Anyway, I hope he's right about Charles Drake, because it would certainly take a load off Mikal's mind."

"Well, right now, I don't think Mikal has but one thought on his mind. Just listen to him. When did you tell him about the baby?"

"Last night after we got home. You should have seen him, Amy. He was like a crazy person. He already has his son's entire future planned for him." Margaret giggled. "I haven't mentioned the fact that he just might have a daughter."

Amy laughed too. "He's had enough surprises for one day. You'd better save that one for later."

Their conversation was interrupted when two women walked into the shop. "What's the joke?" one of them asked. "Tell us so we can laugh too."

Sobering her expression, Amy pushed a stray ringlet off her forehead and tucked it into the braid from which it had escaped. "We're just happy today, Mrs. Crowder. I'm so glad to have Margaret back. And wait until you see the new merchandise she brought with her, straight from New York."

Mrs. Crowder's countenance lit up with a smile that accented the many creases in her heavily powdered face. "No wonder you're happy, Dear. Look, Vivian, our Margaret is back. Now I can talk to her about that hat I'll be needing."

While Margaret discussed Mrs. Crowder's new hat with her, Amy showed Mrs. Hayslip some of the new fabrics on the shelf and flipped through the pages of *Godey's Lady's Book* to show her the newest styles. Before the shop closed for the noon hour, two new orders waited to be filled, one for a resplendent hat and the other for an elegant red taffeta ball gown. The two stylish shoppers went home ecstatic.

# four

In the days that followed, the little millinery shop on Market Street continued to buzz with activity. Word had spread throughout the city about the new merchandise available since Margaret's return, and Apalachicola's ladies all seemed to want new hats and gowns for Easter. Books too seemed to be flying off the shelves.

Although it was her custom to hang a "Closed for Business" sign on the front door during the noon hour, lately Amy had worked through the middle of the day without a break. She couldn't very well push customers out the door to suit her own convenience. As a result, she barely found time to tend to her personal needs.

Rachel and Priscilla, the two girls whom Amy had hired to help cut and baste on a part-time basis, were being pressed into service almost every day. In a pinch, Amy could count on them to wait on customers, but only she and Margaret could help the ladies plan new outfits. And of course, Amy wouldn't think of leaving the shop in the hands of the two young girls for any length of time. Neither could read or write, and Amy was uneasy about having them handle money and count out change. It was not their honesty she questioned; it was their mathematical skills.

If only Margaret would come in to help her more. Amy knew Margaret had her hands full at home, unpacking and doing all the things that were part of reopening a house after a long absence. Still, she had been back for more than a week now, and Amy wished for just an hour of respite each day—a little time to call her own.

Early morning hours were her best because the ladies who frequented her shop did not begin to arrive until after the sun had been up for at least two hours. Amy always rose well before first light to cook a pan of oatmeal for Alex before he left to distribute his morning newspapers and to perform her own ablutions.

As soon as he was gone, she took the pitcher from the washstand and poured water into her washbowl to bathe before she dressed. Then came the task of brushing and braiding her long, dark hair. This morning it felt stiff and unmanageable. She simply must find time today to wash her hair beneath the backyard pump. If she could close the shop during the noon hour, she just might have time to wash her hair and dry it in the sunshine before time to reopen again.

Market Street seemed to come to life by eight o'clock. Amy could hear the *clip-clop* of horses' hooves as they beat against the dirt street and the shouts of merchants setting up for their business of the day.

Amy picked up a needle and thread to put the finishing touches on Mrs. Winslow's ball gown. She had only to hem it and add a row of ruching to the bertha. She smiled, remembering that what Mrs. Winslow had really desired was to have a bustle attached; but according to her report, Mr. Winslow had said he absolutely refused to take her out if she wore one of those "monstrous packs on her back." Amy had tried to mollify the woman's disappointment by adding a large, fat satin bow in place of the bustle.

"Good morning!"

Amy was surprised at the greeting because she hadn't heard the doorbell tinkle, but there stood Margaret with her sleeves pushed up, ready to work.

"Oh, Margaret! I am so glad to see you." Amy laid her work aside and moved to give her friend a hug. "We've been so busy since you brought all those new fabrics and books, and people are still crowding around for a look at that thing you call a sewing machine."

"Have you used it yet, Amy? I hope it will prove to be a wise investment."

Amy knew her sheepish look must have given away her answer even before she admitted, "No, I haven't tried to use it yet. At least, not for a real work job. I have to confess I'm still a little afraid to trust it. But give me some time, and I'll get the hang of it. A few of the ladies have come in to buy quarter-yard pieces of fabric just to have me run a row of the chain stitch for them to take home and show their family and friends. One even suggested she might like a row of the stitching to trim one of her aprons."

Margaret laughed. "Well, that's not what I had in mind when I talked Mikal into buying it for the shop, but perhaps that's a way to start getting people used to the idea." She stashed her reticule beneath the counter and hung her sweater on a hook. "I'm so sorry I haven't been in here to help you more this week, Amy. The truth is, I haven't been feeling well these mornings when I first wake up. And I can't seem to stay awake long enough to get anything done."

Amy glanced up in alarm. "Oh, I hope you're not—" Then, when realization hit her, she said, "Oh, of course. I guess those symptoms are natural when you're carrying a child. But the sickness probably won't last long. Take care of yourself, and don't worry about things here in the shop. Just come in whenever you can, because I can surely use all the help I can get right now."

At that moment, the first customers came through the door, and Margaret moved forward to wait on them while Amy picked up her needle and thread and resumed her sewing.

Both Amy and Margaret were kept busy through the rest of the morning; but by the noon hour, things had begun to slow down a mite. "Margaret, I simply can't go another day without washing my hair. I think I'll try to lock up for an hour today. Why don't you go home and take a nap? You really do look a little pale."

"I'm fine," Margaret assured her, "but a nap does sound appealing. Go ahead and get started on your hair. I'll stay and lock up. Then, if I can make myself wake up, I'll be back to help you after dinner."

"Are you sure you—?"

"Scoot! Get out of here before someone else comes in. I'll hang the sign on the door before I leave."

Amy gave her a grateful smile before she went upstairs to get her soap and towel.

ça

Charles Drake tried to turn the knob on the door of the millinery shop before he noticed the sign hanging against the glass pane: Closed for Business until One O'clock. He looked at the sun overhead and judged it to be about high noon, which meant he would have to wait an hour before he could deliver his message.

Remembering the pump around back where he had found cool, clear water on his first visit to the shop, he rounded the corner of the building to quench his thirst. Was it only a week ago that Amy had given him a plate of nourishing corn bread and beans? That food had tasted like a meal fit for a king. He wasn't sure how much longer he could have stayed on his feet without something to eat that day. What stroke of luck had led him to Amy's shop?

Amy. He had thought of little else since their last encounter. Yet he had no right to think of her at all. Why would a fine lady like Amy give a moment's thought to a man like him, a beggar in ragged clothes?

But today, thanks to the kindness and generosity of Mikal Lee, he wore clothes with no tears or holes. And he remembered telling Amy that he was not a beggar in the true sense of the word.

In better days, he might have had something worthwhile to offer a refined and genteel woman, but that was before tragedy had struck his life and changed it forever. Now all he had left was a heart full of revenge and a score to settle.

And then, of course, he had Melinda to think about. She had cried when he left, and his heart ached for her suffering. He hated leaving her, but he had no choice. He had promised her he would return, and that was a promise he intended to keep.

As he rounded the corner of the building, he stopped short. There beside the pump sat a woman who looked for all the world like Amy. He stood still and watched for a few seconds, spellbound. It *was* Amy. Today, instead of a crown of braids circling her head, a flowing mane of dark hair floated around her shoulders, hanging all the way down to her waist.

In dreams he had imagined what she would look like with her hair down, but this reality surpassed all his dreams. She was even more beautiful than he remembered.

She looked up and saw him. Her cheeks turned a flaming red. Her voice echoed the displeasure that blazed from her eyes. "Charles! What are you doing here? How dare you sneak up to spy on me this way!"

"P–please. . . ," he stammered, groping for words. "It was not my intention to surprise you. I merely came to, um. . ." For a brief moment, he almost forgot his purpose in coming. Then he remembered. "I came to deliver a message from Mikal Lee; but when I saw the sign on your door, I decided to come back here to your pump for a drink of water while I waited. I'm so sorry if I startled you." He hadn't moved, afraid she would bolt if he approached; yet he was reluctant to turn away from the sight of her. "Will you forgive me?"

"There's nothing to forgive," she assured him, as her face recaptured its normal color. "I've just washed my hair. If you'll give me a few moments to run upstairs and make myself presentable, I'll unlock the front door and let you in."

Charles wanted to tell her she was already presentable in his mind. In fact, she was more than presentable. She was ravishing. But of course, he couldn't tell her any of that. "I'll wait on the front steps. Take whatever time you need."

Amy picked up her towel and her rose-scented lye soap from a flat rock close to the pump. With her hairbrush and her key in her hand, she slipped past him and disappeared around the corner of the building.

To Charles, these last few minutes seemed almost like a dream. He had thought of her so much during the week since they'd met; and now their real-life encounter was over almost before it began, leaving him to wonder if it had really happened at all.

He walked around the building and sat on the top step, stretching his long legs toward the sidewalk. Yes, he'd wait here for her. For whatever time it took, he'd wait.

Several pedestrians passed by on the sidewalk and gave Charles a questioning stare, but no one stopped to talk. He watched a horse-drawn carriage roll by, its passengers giving not even a sideways glance at him.

At last he heard the click of the front door latch. "Come in, Charles. I am curious to hear the message from Mikal Lee. I hope it doesn't have anything to do with his wife's health. She left here feeling very tired this morning."

Charles came to his feet and entered the shop. To his disappointment, Amy now had her hair tightly secured into a crown of braids. Only a few errant tendrils had escaped, falling on her forehead in enchanting wisps of dark ringlets.

"No, nothing like that. He's still strutting around telling anyone who'll listen about the new son he's expecting." Charles laughed, but then he remembered his real mission. Reaching into his pocket, he pulled out a small white bulb and placed it on the counter.

"What's that?" Amy asked. She picked it up and examined

it. "Why, it just looks like plain old garlic. Why would Mikal send me garlic? Is this some kind of joke?"

"It almost seems like a joke," Charles admitted, "but the word around the waterfront is that if you wear a clove of this in your shoe every day, it can keep you from getting yellow fever." Seeing Amy's skeptical look, he added, "It doesn't make much sense to me, either; but if there's any chance at all that it works, it's sure worth a try. From what we hear, a real epidemic of yellow fever has hit the town of Saint Joseph, and that's scarcely thirty miles away." He lifted up one foot and pointed to his worn brogans. "I might as well admit I put some garlic in my own shoes this morning. Mikal did too, and he took some home to Margaret. He wants you to use it for yourself and for Alex."

"Oh, we will, Charles. Tell Mikal that Alex and I will each wear a clove of garlic in our shoes, and we do thank him for letting us know. If wearing garlic in our shoes doesn't work to ward off yellow fever, at least it doesn't hurt anything. We must all take every possible precaution against that deadly disease."

Charles continued to look at her, reluctant to take his leave. "Was there something else, then?" she asked him finally.

"Um, no, I guess that's about it for now. Unless you have an errand you'd like for me to do." He held his breath, hoping she would think of something to prolong the encounter, but she shook her head.

"Nothing for now, Charles, but I appreciate your delivery of that important message. If you happen to run into Alex this afternoon, please tell him to hurry home, but don't tell him I plan to put garlic in his shoes. He just might take his time about getting here."

Charles chuckled. "Alex is a typical boy, all right. If I see him, I'll personally put a clove of garlic in each of his shoes. How's that?"

Just as he spoke, the bell over the door tinkled; and a tall, white-haired woman entered the shop, capturing Amy's immediate attention.

"Good afternoon, Mrs. Gatewick. How nice to see you today."

Without a parting word, Charles slipped quietly out the door. He didn't want to put Amy in the embarrassing position of having to answer questions about his visit to her shop. He could only wish for the very best of success for this kind, charming woman; and try as he might, he could not see how he could ever fit into that picture.

## five

With Easter fast approaching, Amy stayed so busy that she had little time to ponder about the stranger from the red hills; and she was sure he must have forgotten about her by now. She had neither seen nor heard from him since the day they'd met by the backyard pump.

The sound of scissors seldom stopped in the little shop, as Rachel and Priscilla cut into the luxurious fabrics chosen by the ladies of Apalachicola for their Easter finery. Margaret too had been faithful about coming in every day to wait on customers and turn out her fancy bonnets and hats in preparation for the big day.

Amy faithfully wore cloves of garlic in her shoes each day and made sure Alex did likewise, even though no cases of yellow fever had been reported within the town's boundaries.

According to the local newspaper, the port of Saint Joseph had been placed under quarantine; and it was hoped that somehow the spread of the dreadful disease could be stopped before it reached any farther.

Local panic seemed to have subsided. Mr. Diamanti's general store had once again replenished its recently depleted supply of garlic bulbs, and things seemed to have returned to a semblance of normalcy.

On a balmy April afternoon, Amy crouched on her knees, pinning the hem in Mrs. Gatewick's green silk gown. "Turn just a little more to the right, Mrs. Gatewick." Amy spoke through pinched lips, trying to keep the pins from dropping to the floor. "There, that should do it."

She was caught in this position when Alex burst into the

room. "Mama," he shouted, "Mr. Mikal told me to come quick to tell y'all that he just got word President Harrison died yesterday."

Everyone in the room froze in shocked silence. Margaret was the first to speak. "Can this be true? Oh, my. Mikal was so optimistic President Harrison would hasten the Florida Territory's admission to the United States. I wonder what will happen now."

"But he's only been president for a month!" Amy exclaimed. "Why, I was just reading about his inauguration. What a tragedy for the country."

A teardrop rolled down Mrs. Gatewick's cheek and landed on her new gown, forming a dark spot on the skirt. "Let's get you out of this and finish the hem tomorrow," Amy suggested, loosening the fasteners down her back.

"Oh, yes, please do," the lady agreed. "I can't think about clothes right now. All I can think of is that poor Anna Harrison. I heard she was lovely in her inaugural gown last month. I'm sure this must be devastating for her."

"You want me to take back any message?" Alex asked, standing in the doorway. Amy had forgotten about her young son, who had delivered the shocking news. She turned to him, stricken. "No, except to let Mr. Mikal know we appreciate his thoughtfulness in sending us word. And thank you, Son, for running to bring us the sad news."

The shop cleared out quickly after that. Like Mrs. Gatewick, no one had a mind on clothes. "We might as well lock up for the day," Amy decided. "Perhaps we should make a wreath to hang on our door." She lifted the green gown from the table where it lay in a crumpled heap and hung it on a hanger, using her fingers to smooth out the wrinkles. She hoped the tiny spot on the skirt would disappear when it dried.

"Amy," Margaret began, "I'm glad we can have a few moments alone, because I need to talk to you about something."

Amy's heart suddenly felt like a lead weight. She knew by Margaret's tone of voice that what she was about to hear was not good news. She stopped and stood stock-still, waiting for Margaret's next words.

"Oh, don't look so worried," her friend assured her. "It's not really bad news. I just wanted to give you plenty of notice that Mikal and I will be leaving again soon after Easter. I wanted you to have time to plan ahead."

"Margaret," Amy gasped. "You can't be serious."

"Oh, Amy, I hate to leave so much on your shoulders; but this may be the last time I'll be able to go with Mikal on his trips to New York, at least for awhile."

"What are you thinking?" Amy lifted both hands in despair and looked Margaret square in the eye. "I can't imagine you'd make such a trip now, in your delicate condition. I can't imagine Mikal allowing you to go. Do you really think this is a wise decision?"

Margaret screwed up her face and rubbed her eyes. "I've given it a lot of thought, Amy. I really have." Then a smile began to play on her lips. "I'm going to need lots of things for our new baby, and New York has so much to offer."

"Yes, but—"

"And another thing, Amy. Even though I know it's a popular expression, I refuse to think of my condition as 'delicate,' when I don't feel delicate at all. Dr. John says I'm in perfect health, and he doesn't think the trip will cause any problems. Mikal's already talked to him about it, and you know how close Mikal is to John Gorrie. They're like brothers. He knows John wouldn't encourage me to go if he had even the slightest misgivings."

Amy turned away and pulled a broom from the closet. As she swept up the ravels and threads from beneath the cutting tables, she kept her silence. She remembered the hard work and long hours during Margaret's last absence.

Without extra help, could she really keep the orders filled and the discriminating clientele satisfied? And besides all the work, there was the loneliness.

Perhaps it was her own fault that Margaret was her only close friend. She loved the ladies of her church, but most of them had husbands and children to care for. As far as Amy knew, not one of them worked outside the home. Beyond a quick smile and a few kind words, these women had little time for a working woman. No, whenever Amy needed another woman to talk to, there was only Margaret.

Amy pushed the pile of snips and scraps onto a dustpan and deposited it in the trash can.

"Don't look so downhearted, Amy," Margaret begged. "It's only for a couple of months, and I'll be back to help well before the Christmas season." She walked around the table to give her friend a hug. "Be happy for me. I'll bring back lots of new ideas for the holidays."

Yes, Amy thought. Ideas about baby quilts and booties and things. She might as well get used to the idea of running the shop alone because, as things stood now, she wasn't likely to get much help from Margaret anytime in the near future.

A sharp rap on the front door broke up the awkward moment, and Amy put down her broom and straightened her skirt. "I guess I shouldn't have locked the door. Probably not everyone has heard about the president's death, or perhaps some are not as moved by the news as we are."

As she unlocked the door and opened it, she was almost knocked off her feet by the sour-faced matron who barged in, dragging a little girl by the hand. "Why, Mrs. Simpson, how nice—"

"You'd better not say how nice until you hear what I have to tell you. I have just about had a enough of that ill-mannered son of yours. Where is he anyway?" She turned in a complete circle to scan the room for her victim, while her little girl stood beside her, trying hard to hold onto her mother's skirts.

"Alex? What in the world has he done?" As Amy's mouth gaped in shock, Margaret stepped to her side in a show of support. Both ladies looked in amazement at the irate Mrs. Simpson.

"I'll tell you what he's done," she shrieked. "He's done everything he can to torture my sweet little Mattilou, hasn't he, Darling?" She pulled her daughter from behind her skirt and thrust her in front to face the two women. "He is making my daughter's life miserable. Tell them what Alex said."

Mattilou tried to retreat, but her mother held her fast. "Tell them, I said."

The plump little girl tossed her long brown curls. "I–I can't remember," she stammered. But after a not-so-gentle push from behind, she said, "He–he called me 'Fatti-lou.'"

Amy was shocked. "My Alex said that?" When Mattilou nodded in the affirmative, Amy tried to comfort her. "My dear, I am so sorry. I will speak to him the minute he gets home."

"Speak to him! That's all you're going to do to him?" Mrs. Simpson's face turned purple with anger. "Just wait until I get my hands on him. I'll do more than speak to him. I–I'll—"

"You'll do what, Mrs. Simpson?" Margaret stepped between Amy and her accuser. "I've been around Alex enough to know that, even though at times he's a mischievous little boy, he's not ill-mannered as you said; and if he's done something wrong, I'm sure his mother will take whatever steps necessary to see it doesn't happen again."

"Hmph! If his mother was a normal woman who stayed home and took care of her child instead of sending him out on the streets while she works in a shop all day—"

"I think quite enough has been said for today," Margaret declared. "Here, Mattilou, have a peppermint stick." She picked up a candy stick from a dish on the counter and handed it to the child.

Mattilou's round cheeks broke into a wide smile as her chubby fingers reached eagerly for the treat, but her mother snatched it from her grasp and threw it on the floor. Glaring at Amy, she added, "It's going to take more than a few sweets to make me forget about this, Mrs. McCutcheon. You haven't heard the last from me." Dragging her daughter by the hand, she marched toward the door. "Come, Mattilou."

Amy covered her face with both hands. "Oh, Margaret, what am I going to do? It's so hard to be both mother and father to Alex. I can't imagine what possessed him to do such a mean thing. And Mrs. Simpson is right. I really don't have enough time to spend with my son. I don't want him to grow up to be a wicked man." She used her fingers to wipe the tears running down her cheeks.

Margaret put an arm around her shoulders. "Amy, don't you think you should wait and hear Alex's side of the story before you pass judgment? Granted, he probably said something he shouldn't have, and I'm sure you'll straighten him out about that, but Mattilou must have done something to provoke such an action. Alex is so kindhearted; I can't imagine him deliberately trying to hurt someone."

"What else can happen this day?" Amy wondered aloud. "Mrs. Simpson's vindictive nature is well-known, and I shudder to think how she might try to avenge Alex's misbehavior. Oh, I just wish I could wake up and start this day all over again."

"Yes, well, we both know that's not possible. Just try to lean on the Lord for guidance, and He will show you the way. Let's pray about it before I leave you."

Margaret held Amy's hands as they bowed their heads. "Lord Jesus, please give Amy the patience, the strength, and the wisdom to deal with the problems this day has brought her. Let her feel Thy loving arms around her as she seeks to do Thy will. In Jesus' name we pray. Amen."

"Thank you, Margaret. I feel better already," Amy said. "I'll let you know tomorrow how everything works out."

Pausing at the threshold, Margaret turned back and winked playfully. "Just remember, Amy. This is the day that the Lord has made. We should rejoice and be glad in it."

Amy locked the door behind her and finished tidying the shop for another busy day tomorrow. Alex would be home soon. What would he have to say for himself? And what would she say in return?

# six

"I didn't start it," Alex protested. "Mattilou started it herself. She always follows us boys around trying to start something. She calls us lots of bad names—lots worse than what we say to her. We just want her to leave us alone."

Amy rolled her eyes heavenward. What could she do to make Alex understand? "It doesn't matter who started it. You know better than to call someone a derogatory name." With one hand on his shoulder, she shook her forefinger in his face and used her sternest tone. Somehow she had to get through to him.

"I never called her that, Mama. Honest. I don't even know what a roggy torry is. All I said was—"

"I know what you said, Alex, and I don't want to hear it again. Mrs. Simpson made sure Mattilou told me all about it, and you should be ashamed. Don't you remember what we read in the Bible about how we're supposed to treat others as we would want to be treated?"

"Yes, Ma'am." Alex hung his head and focused his eyes on a spot on the floor. "I won't call her Fatti, um, that name, not ever again. I promise. Can I go now?"

Amy heaved a sigh of exasperation. "No, Alex, you may not go anywhere except upstairs to your cot, and there'll be no supper for you tonight. Tomorrow you must find Mattilou and apologize to her."

When Alex jerked his head up, his face was a reflection of pure horror. "No, Ma. I can't do that. Please don't make me do that. The other fellows will laugh at me and call me a sissy. I'll go without supper, and I'll do anything you say, but please don't make me apologize to that—that silly, high-falutin—"

"Alex!" Apparently he had not learned his lesson at all. "Go straight to bed this minute. We'll talk about this again later. For now, I need a breath of fresh air to clear my head. I declare, you've put me in a dither. I'm going down to the general store to pick up some groceries, and I want you to stay on your cot and meditate on how naughty you've been."

She watched him shuffle up the stairs, his head hung low. Whenever she punished him, she felt the hurt herself, all the way down to her toes. She did love him so, but she absolutely must turn him into a decent citizen, and she couldn't allow him to insult little girls, even if they were, well, a bit silly and highfalutin.

She pulled her cloak from a nail on the wall, picked up her reticule, and started for the store.

The afternoon sun, slung low in the sky, cast a golden glow over the town. Although it was almost a mile from her door to the store, Amy always enjoyed walking down Market Street. Today she needed the time alone to think about how to handle the situation with Alex. He was such a good boy. Meanness was not part of his nature. Whatever the cause, this kind of behavior must be stopped before it became a habit. Perhaps she would ask Mikal to have a word with the boy. A man seemed to know how to deal with these matters better than a woman.

How blessed the new baby would be to live in a home with two loving parents. If she should ever marry again—but of course, she never would—it would be a great comfort, she admitted to herself, to be able to share her problems instead of shouldering them alone.

But she wasn't alone. Hadn't the Lord promised to walk with her? Just last night she had read in her Bible, "Cast thy burden upon the LORD, and He shall sustain thee." *Dear*

*Lord,* she prayed, *please show me the way to lead Alex in the paths of righteousness. And please open his young heart to Your teachings.*

Amy was so engrossed in her prayer that she almost bumped headlong into two ladies coming from the general store, their arms filled with packages. "Oh, excuse me. I wasn't watching where I'm going," Amy apologized.

The ladies quickly recovered. "No harm done," one assured her. "But if you're going to the general store, you might want to think twice and decide to go home and come back tomorrow instead."

Amy looked in the direction of the store. She was almost there, and she needed several items before the morrow. "Why? Is there some kind of problem?"

"Oh, it's just disgraceful," the first lady offered, and her friend was quick to add her comments.

"In broad daylight, a drunk staggering around on the porch. Mr. Diamanti has probably already had him arrested by now, but do be careful, Dear. Apalachicola used to be such a nice city, but lately we see more and more of these vagrants roaming our streets."

The two shoppers hurried on, and Amy hesitated for just a few moments. She did not care to encounter any unpleasantness, yet she did need her supplies. As she drew closer to the store, she saw that a small crowd had clustered in the street, laughing and pointing. Two steps closer, she could see the object of their ridicule. A tall, sandy-haired man was indeed staggering, clutching at the posts to keep from falling down. He stumbled to the floor, then dragged himself up again and tried to move forward.

The group in the street laughed and jeered at him. "Gettin' an early start on the corn juice, ain'tcha, Feller?"

Amy had almost decided to turn back and return home after all, when she recognized the man on the porch. *Charles*

*Drake!* What a disgusting spectacle he was making of himself! And how disappointing to learn he was a common drunk. More than disappointing, the thought was heart wrenching. Yet as though drawn by a magnet, she went forward, step by hesitant step until she was standing beside him. "Oh, Charles, why have you—?"

But before she finished her sentence, she saw the perspiration that ran down his face and soaked his shirt, saw his mottled cheeks and his anguished eyes. She tentatively reached out with one hand and held it lightly to his forehead. Why, he was burning up with fever! This man wasn't drunk; he was sick.

Amy screamed at the crowd. "Someone help me here. This man is burning up with fever. We must get him to Dr. Gorrie's office at once."

Her words struck a chord of fear in the growing crowd. They moved as one, not forward to help the poor, sick man, but backward into the street.

*"Fever!"* The cry went up, and in minutes the street was clear. Behind her, Amy heard the doors to the general store close and lock. She was alone on the porch with Charles Drake, a very sick man.

Once again she cried for help, but only silence surrounded her. She took one of his long, limp arms and placed it around her shoulder. He must weigh at least twice as much as she did, and she wasn't sure she could support him; but she couldn't just walk off and leave him here alone to die.

"Charles, you've got to try to help me," she pleaded. "Just lean on me and put one foot in front of the other. Dr. Gorrie lives right around the corner. We must find a way to get you there."

Charles had not spoken a word since she found him, but now he groaned a single word of protest. "No."

"Yes, Charles. You must try. You can't stay here. No one

here will help you. If you can make it to John Gorrie's door, he'll see you. I know he will. He never turns anyone away who needs help."

His silence indicated he was too weak to protest; but when Charles shifted his weight from the post to Amy's shoulder, she almost collapsed under his heaviness. *Dear Lord, please give me the strength to help this man.*

Amy tried to visualize Jesus on the other side of Charles, sharing her heavy burden; and although it took all the strength she could muster, they began to inch forward. With each torturous step, she was sure she would fall; but miraculously, they continued to move.

In what seemed to Amy like hours, at last she stood in front of the gate to Dr. Gorrie's home and office with Charles dangling from her shoulders. "Cold," he muttered. He had begun to shake and shudder as a severe chill wracked his body, and Amy could hear the rattle of his teeth.

"Help!" she screamed. "Please, someone. We need help."

Amy recognized the gigantic black man who hurried down the front walk to meet them. "Oh, William, I am so glad you are here. This man has a raging fever, and now he's suffering a severe chill. He needs immediate attention. Is the doctor in?"

William stepped through the gate and shifted Charles from Amy's shoulder onto his own. "You shouldn't ought to be doing this, Miss Amy. Don't you know better than to get around somebody that's got a fever? You need to get yourself as far away from this man as you can. Now, you run on now, you hear me? I'll get him into one of the beds, and Dr. Gorrie, he'll look at him soon as he gets back."

Amy's heart sank. "Are you telling me the doctor is not here? How long will he be away?"

"I don't be knowin' that, 'cause he's makin' his house calls. And Miss Caroline, she be in South Carolina visiting with some of her family. The doctor, he wants for her to stay away 'til this yellow fever business dies down. But don't you be worryin' none. I'll take care of this man. You best be thinkin' about your ownself, Miss Amy."

Amy shook her head. "I'm not leaving, William—not until I'm sure Dr. Gorrie sees to this man. His name is Charles Drake. If you can get him into a bed, I'll sponge him with cool water and try to get his fever down."

Charles hung on William's shoulder like a limp rag doll, ready to fall in the dirt if William released his grip. But William did not let go. Instead, he picked the man up in his arms as though he were a child and carried him into the house.

Amy was just two steps behind him all the way, and William continued to plead with her. "Please, Miss Amy. You can't come in here. You get on home and wipe yourself down good with vinegar."

Amy didn't even slow down, but she raised her eyebrows and asked a question. "Is that what the doctor prescribes? Vinegar?"

"No, Ma'am. The doctor, he don't cotton to that kind of treatment; but I hear other folks say vinegar keeps the ole yellow jack from your door. That and garlic."

They crossed the foyer and stood at the foot of the staircase. William, still holding his patient, made one more effort to send her away. "Please, Miss Amy, if Dr. John comes home and sees I've let you in here with this sick man, he's likely gonna be mighty upset. Besides, I'm gonna take this fellow upstairs and pull off all these wet clothes and put him into a dry gown. You have to stay out."

Amy felt the heat rising to her face. "Of course, William. I'll stay downstairs until you get him dressed and settled; but then, if you'll bring me a rag and a pan of cool water, I want to try to bring down his fever before the doctor gets here."

Amy could hear William muttering all the way up the staircase. "Dr. John, he ain't gonna like this. No sirree, not one little bit."

And William was right. When John Gorrie arrived at his home two hours later and found Amy crouched at the bedside of a very sick man, he boomed in a voice that shook his short, stocky frame. "Amy McCutcheon, have you lost your mind?"

Amy jumped, but she continued to dip her rag into the basin of cool water and squeeze it out to sponge the face and limbs of Charles Drake. "Oh, John. I'm so glad you're here. This is Charles Drake. He's a—a newcomer in town. He works for Mikal down at the waterfront. He's been living in a room in Mikal's warehouse, and I've come to think of him as a—a friend. He collapsed in front of the general store, and I brought him here because I knew you'd help him."

The doctor gripped Amy's arm and pulled her up and away from the bedside. He gentled his tone, sounding more like the kind man she knew him to be. "Amy, you've done a very dangerous thing, considering the risk of possibly exposing yourself to yellow fever."

*Yellow fever!* The dreaded words struck fear in her heart. She'd known all along that this was a strong possibility, but she had hoped and prayed for a less deadly diagnosis. "Is that what he has, then? Are you sure?"

John Gorrie, with his back to her, had already begun to examine the patient. "No, Amy, I can't be sure of a diagnosis at this point. From the looks of him, I'd say he has either yellow fever or malaria. You'd better pray for the latter because, although malaria is a terrible malady, we can dose him up with quinine, and we just might be able to pull him through."

Amy considered the grim alternative. "And if it's the other. . .disease?" She couldn't bring herself to voice its name. "What then?"

John only shook his head. "You'll have to step outside the room now, Amy, but don't go outdoors."

What did he mean about not going outdoors? Amy thought that was exactly what they'd been asking her to do.

Now suddenly he wanted her to stay here. She didn't understand. "You want me to stay?"

"It isn't a matter of what I want. If I determine this man has yellow fever, this house will be under quarantine, with a yellow flag flying out front to warn others. Of course, as a doctor, I have immunity from the quarantine rules, because I'll still have to make the rounds of my homebound patients. But you, young lady, have placed yourself in a very dangerous position."

For the first time since leaving her shop, Amy suddenly thought of Alex, at home in his bed, alone. "My son. . . ," she started to protest.

"You should have thought about that sooner. We'll have to worry about that later, Amy. Right now, I want you to go downstairs and wait until I call you. If need be, I can go out later and find someone to see to your son; but for the moment, my concern is with this patient, and you, my dear, are in my way."

Properly chagrined, Amy made a hasty departure from the room and scurried down the staircase. What kind of situation had she gotten herself into? What would happen to Alex when he discovered she was gone? And overshadowing all other questions was one overriding concern: What was wrong with Charles Drake?

## seven

Amy heard the clock in the hall chime ten bells. How long had she been sitting here in John Gorrie's parlor, waiting for news of Charles's condition? William had tried to coax her into eating a bowl of oyster stew, but the very thought of food nauseated her. "Just a glass of cool water, please," she had told him, and he had answered her request with a pitcher of water and a tall crystal glass on a silver tray.

Although she could hear the kind servant in the kitchen, rattling pots and pans, he respected her wish to be alone with her thoughts.

What could possibly be taking John so long to get back to her with at least a preliminary report? Was Charles hanging on to the fragile thread of life, or was he slipping away into eternity? Amy shuddered as a chill wracked her body when she considered the grim possibility of Charles's demise. How had he become so important to her in such a short time? Only the remembrance of John's scalding words about being in the way kept her from going back upstairs. If she could just stand outside the bedroom door and listen for the reassuring sound of Charles's breathing, she would ask for no more for the moment.

When a knock on the front door broke into her thoughts, she heard William coming to answer it. Although she couldn't see into the foyer, she recognized the familiar voice of Mikal Lee. "William, is John available?"

"No, Sir, Mr. John be upstairs with a patient; and I'm sorry, Mr. Mikal, but he told me not to let nobody come through this door. I hate to say that to you, 'cause I know you be his best friend and all, but—"

"Mikal!" Amy was on her feet, rushing toward the door before William restrained her. "Let go of me, William. I need to talk to Mikal. I must!"

"William, what's going on here?" Mikal demanded. "Why can't I come in?"

The old servant tried to explain. "Miss Amy, she brought a sick man in here this afternoon, and the doctor won't let nobody in or out 'til he figures out what ails him."

"It's all right, William." From the top of the staircase, John Gorrie leaned against the newel post and called down to them. "Let him in. I'm on my way down to give you my diagnosis." His slow, faltering steps revealed his exhaustion.

Amy felt suddenly light-headed. Hours of tension coupled with a lack of food were taking their toll, but she willed herself not to faint. She had to be strong for Charles. *Dear Lord, please let this be good news!* Part of her wanted to push John for quick answers, but another part of her stood in dread of what she might hear.

"Let's all go in the parlor and sit down," John said, taking a handkerchief from his pocket and mopping his brow. "William, would you bring us some coffee, please?"

"What's this about a sick man?" Mikal wanted to know.

Amy told him in as few words as possible how she came to be there and how she had brought Charles Drake to the doctor's home with an unknown illness. "I'll tell you the details later, Mikal. But first, let's hear what John can tell us."

"First things first," the doctor said with tantalizing torpidity. "To answer the question uppermost in your minds, I do not believe this man has yellow fever."

Amy exhaled audibly, her shoulders crumpling in relief. *Thank You, Lord!* She listened while John continued.

"He appears to have a bad case of malaria. Well, there's no

such thing as a *good* case of malaria," he quipped. "But it's usually not as serious as yellow fever. I've reduced his body temperature with my cooling apparatus and given him a hefty dose of quinine, so he's resting comfortably at the moment. But I'll need to keep an eye on him. Malaria can be tricky and sometimes fatal, but I believe after a few days here with my machinery and William's nourishing broths, we'll be able to bring this man around. Who is he, anyway?"

"He's a newcomer to town," Mikal explained. "He hails from the red hills north of us." Mikal ignored John's raised eyebrows at the mention of the red hills. "I've given him a job and a place to live. He seems to be a well-bred man who's down on his luck, but I'll tell you this: He's a hard worker."

John sat with his hands clasped in his lap and nodded. "I can believe that by the way he is fighting this illness. A lesser man would have given up before now." He picked up his cup and sipped from the steaming coffee William had placed before him. "Amy, I know you're anxious to get home to your son, but it's pretty late for a lady to be out on the streets alone."

"Not a problem," Mikal assured him. "I'll walk the lady home and see her safely to her door." He rose to his feet, leaving his coffee untouched. "I'll have coffee with you again another time, John. I can see Amy is anxious to go."

Amy had already fastened the shawl around her shoulders and was standing by the door. "Thank you so much, John. I'm sorry I caused you concern tonight, but I had to find help, and I knew you'd know what to do for my. . .for Mr. Drake. I'll stop by in the morning to see how he's faring."

Mikal and John exchanged glances. "You do that, Amy. I'll continue to cool him when his fever rises; and if he survives the night, we should be able to see some improvement by morning."

Mikal held the front door open for Amy and followed her out into the night.

❧

Amy needn't have worried. Alex was sleeping soundly when she got home. She straightened his quilt and kissed him lightly on the forehead, but he did not stir.

As tired as she felt, Amy knew she wouldn't be able to sleep right away. Her emotions were too taut. She made herself a cup of sassafras tea sweetened with a teaspoon of molasses and sat down to read her Bible by candlelight.

*Casting all your care upon Him; for He careth for you.* Amy thought she had been casting quite a lot on the Lord lately, and she gave thanks that He cared for her. He cared for Alex too, and for Charles Drake as well.

Then she turned the pages to the seventh chapter of Matthew and read the verses where Jesus had taught His disciples to treat others as they would wish to be treated. Tomorrow she would have to talk to Alex about his consideration of others and insist that he apologize to Mattilou. That was sure to be a difficult lesson for him, but she hoped it would be one he long remembered.

Granted, Mattilou's mother had a reputation as a trouble-maker, and by all accounts, her daughter seemed to be following in her footsteps; but Alex had been wrong to participate in teasing the little girl. He would have to accept his punishment as a bitter medicine to be swallowed. Amy just hoped the medicine would be strong enough to effect a cure.

Amy tried to dismiss the vicious threat Mrs. Simpson had snarled at her as she left the shop: "You haven't heard the last from me." The woman was upset. Surely she would not carry as a grudge the misdeed of a child, and yet. . .

With all the problems of this day, and in spite of her best efforts to divert them, her thoughts kept turning back to the man who lay struggling for his life in John Gorrie's bed.

It was while she had been sponging Charles Drake's tanned and muscled shoulders to bring down his fever that she suddenly realized how strong her feelings for him had become. How could she develop such sentiment for a man about whom she knew so little? What had brought him from the infamous red hills to the gulf shores of Apalachicola? Was he even a Christian? She had no right to have any special feelings for this man who was virtually a stranger; yet, as she had ministered to his needs, she felt a strong attraction that seemed beyond her control. These emotions were all new and strange to Amy, but they were so powerful that she wondered if God might have His hand in gently nudging her down this untried path. So many questions, all without answers.

Tomorrow she would walk to John Gorrie's house and inquire about Charles Drake's physical condition. She prayed she would find him much improved, and with just a little luck, perhaps she might even find an answer to some of her questions. Today she had only done what any Christian would have done. There was nothing more she could do for him tonight.

She closed her Bible, blew out her candle, and went to bed.

# eight

Charles Drake opened his eyes and wondered for a moment where he was and how he had come to be there. He remembered becoming ill on his way to the general store, and he recalled people laughing at him, believing him to be drunk.

No, he hadn't been drunk—never had been, in fact. He'd seen the results of whiskey while he was growing up and had decided at an early age that he wanted nothing to do with it. But of course, the people who saw him had no way of knowing that, and he had been too sick to tell them. Too sick to care what they thought. Was that only yesterday, or was it weeks ago? He had lost all sense of time.

He recalled that someone had tried to help him. Someone soft and small. In his delirium, he had imagined it was Amy; but of course it couldn't have been. If she had witnessed that scene, she would have been as thoroughly repulsed by his behavior as the rest of the people had been. No, it couldn't have been Amy; but then who?

His memory was fuzzy. He had drifted in and out of consciousness. After a long struggle to remain on his feet, he recalled being lifted at last by strong arms and carried up a staircase. He'd been gently placed on a bed with cool, clean sheets. Only then had he been able to relax his struggle and give way to the comforting darkness that claimed him.

Later there were soft, sensitive hands that bathed him with cool water. Again he dreamed that Amy was near, but of course that was simply another manifestation of his delirium. It was only natural he should think of her in his time of need, since he had thought of little else since the day he first set eyes on her.

If only he were free to let her know how much he admired her, he would have done so long ago. But he had forced himself to relegate Amy to his world of dreams; and in fairness to her, that was as close as he could ever allow her to be.

All night long he had alternated between body-wracking chills and searing-hot fever. Once—or was it twice?—strong arms had lifted him and changed him from a hot, soaking-wet gown into one that was cool and dry. His sheets too had been changed during the night. Someone had gone to a great deal of effort to make him comfortable. But who?

His eyes scanned the room, seeking an answer to his questions. A strange whirring sound drew his attention to the corner of the room where, suspended from the ceiling, whirling blades of metal stirred the air and sent currents of wind over a basin of ice on the floor. The refreshing draft washed over him, cooling his feverish body. He had never seen such a contraption. He tried to lift his head for a better look, but his head spun like a weather vane in a hurricane and dropped onto his pillow.

"Feeling better, are we?" The man standing over his bed looked vaguely familiar. Charles had seen him at the waterfront talking to Mikal. "You've given us quite a scare, young man. I'm John Gorrie, your doctor, and I must say you look a lot better than you did yesterday when you came in here."

Charles wrinkled his brow and tried to remember. "What happened to me? Is this a hospital?"

John chuckled. "One question at a time, please. Yes, this is a hospital. It's also my home, my office, my laboratory, or whatever else you might want to call it. As to what happened to you, you became ill and might have died had it not been for a very brave little lady."

"Yes, I think I remember something about that. Who was she? I must thank her when I'm able."

"Her name is Amy McCutcheon," John said. "You may be able to thank her sooner than you imagine because William tells me she's in my parlor waiting to get an update on your health." He leaned over and placed his stethoscope on Charles's chest. "Breathe deeply, please."

Charles tried again to raise his head. "Amy is here?"

A gentle push flattened him to the bed. "Has this virus settled in your ears? Didn't you hear me? I said to breathe deeply."

In his weakened condition, Charles had little choice but to do as he was told. He took several deep breaths, but he kept his eyes fastened on the door. Was Amy really here? At last he could restrain his tongue no longer. "Look here, Doctor. Tell me what's wrong with me? Do I have the yellow jack? Because if I do, I sure don't want Amy or anyone else to get near me."

Dr. Gorrie continued listening, thumping, and prodding Charles's body, ignoring his questions until he finished his examination. "No, Charles, I am quite certain that you are not a victim of yellow fever."

"Thank God!"

"Yes, you should thank Him that you're still alive, but don't start celebrating yet. You have a long way to go." John took a small fold of white paper and spooned white powder from a jar into it. "Here, take this." He pushed the paper between Charles's lips and tapped it to make sure he emptied its contents into his patient's mouth. The doctor supported Charles's head while he gave him sips of water from a glass.

Charles shuddered at the bitter taste of the powder but swallowed without protest. "What is that for?" he asked. "You haven't told me what's wrong with me."

"I'm afraid you have malaria. There's a good bit of it going around right now. We don't know what causes it or how to cure it, but we do know that quinine seems to help. And that fan you see blowing cool air on you, that's an invention I'm working on to lower the temperature of my patients. I believe it has been helping you. However, I must warn you, you'll be weak as a kitten for a very long time. When you leave here, you'll have to arrange to have assistance. And this is a crazy illness, because just when you begin to believe you're over it, it recurs, even a year from now and more."

Charles pondered the doctor's words. He had no money to hire a helper. Weak or not, he'd simply have to cope with life on his own. And what about his job? Mikal had given him such a grand opportunity. He couldn't afford to lose it.

The doctor seemed to read his mind. "Don't worry about payment for my services, Charles. When you're able, we'll talk about a schedule to settle your bill; but for now, I want you to concentrate on taking care of yourself."

Even as the kind doctor spoke, Charles could feel himself drifting out of consciousness. He tried to mouth a reply but could not. He was tired. So very tired.

"There's a little lady downstairs who is chomping at the bit to hear my diagnosis, Charles. Perhaps by tomorrow I can allow her to come upstairs and see you for a few moments."

Unable to pull his thoughts into focus enough to understand the doctor's words, Charles closed his eyes and lapsed into an abyss of darkness where neither sight nor sound could penetrate.

❧

Amy paced the floor. She had tried to sit on the sofa in John Gorrie's parlor, but she couldn't relax—not even when William brought her a tray of tea and buttered toast. Her stomach churned in anticipation of the news she waited to hear. Had Charles survived the night? And if so, what was his prognosis?

She strained her ears for sounds, but most of them came from the kitchen where William was busy with his morning chores. She could hear footsteps overhead but not voices. Then at last she heard John descending the stairs, calling her name. "Amy?"

She met him at the bottom of the steps and frantically tried to read his face. "How is he, John? Is he going to get better?"

John touched her gently on the shoulder. "It's going to take some time, Amy, but with the proper care, I believe your gentleman friend will eventually be restored to health."

Relief flooded her body. "Thank you, John." She could no longer restrain the tears that found their way down her cheeks. "I know you will give him the care he needs."

John shook his head. "Now, just a minute, my dear. I'm not in a position to provide extended care for my patients here in the hospital. I have other patients who need my care. I hope in a day or two Charles will be strong enough to be sent home. He'll be very weak, and he'll need help for some time, but he won't need to be hospitalized. Of course, I'll plan to stop in and see him when I make my daily house calls."

"But he has no house," Amy protested. "He has only a small room in Mikal's warehouse. He doesn't even have a kitchen. I haven't been inside it, but I'm sure it's no place for a sick man. And he has no family to care for him. Couldn't you let him stay here until he's strong again?"

John stroked his chin thoughtfully. "I'm sorry, Dear. That is impossible. Just imagine if all of my patients wanted to stay here. I simply couldn't handle it. But I do have a suggestion for you."

"For me?" She hadn't bothered to correct John when he had referred to Charles as her gentleman friend, but perhaps this was the time to explain that Charles was only a casual acquaintance. If he had grown to mean more to her than that, she certainly did not care to proclaim the fact. "What kind of suggestion did you have in mind?"

"This man's recovery will depend largely on the kind of

care he receives in these next crucial weeks. He's going to need a diet of nourishing food—not the kind one finds along the waterfront—and he will need a good deal of encouragement. Perhaps you could look in on him from time to time and offer to help him. I know Mikal and Margaret will want to help too."

Amy didn't remind him that the Lees would soon be leaving on the *Windsong*. Perhaps if John Gorrie let various townspeople know of the need, some of them might offer to help. But she remembered how they had all turned away from her when she'd needed them most. No, Charles shouldn't count on the townspeople to help him.

The whole city was living in terror of sickness these days, and who could blame them? She had heard reports that the people of Saint Joseph were dropping on the streets like flies from the ravages of yellow fever. Malaria, although slightly less deadly, was still not a disease to be taken lightly.

And Charles was a virtual stranger in Apalachicola. He had no friends that she knew of. She had an uneasy suspicion that if anyone were to provide Charles with nourishing food or even encouragement, the responsibilities would likely fall on her shoulders.

Her voice carried little assurance. "John, I don't. . . I–I'll do what I can when the time comes. But for now, I must get back home and open the shop. Customers are probably lined up by the door, wondering what has happened." She drew her shawl around her shoulders and moved toward the door. "Thank you for everything. You are a very kind man."

Just as she reached the front door, John had an afterthought. "Just a minute, Amy. I meant to ask you something."

She turned to see him scratching his head. "Ever hear of anyone named Melinda?"

Amy thought for a few moments. "No, John. I don't believe I know anyone by that name. Why do you ask?"

"Oh, I was just wondering. It's not important. Just that, in his delirium, Charles kept calling that name over and over again. I thought you might know if that's someone we should try to locate to come help him."

Amy felt her heart plummet to her toes. *Melinda! A sweetheart or even a wife, perhaps!* "I—I'm sure I don't know," she stammered. "Perhaps you should ask him." She turned toward the heavy mahogany door.

"Here, let me get that for you." The doctor stepped in front of her and put his hand on the knob. "You're looking a little pale yourself this morning, Amy." He placed his palm on her forehead. "You don't appear to have a fever. Probably just tired. But you'd better take good care of yourself. These are trying times, and you mustn't let your resistance falter."

"Yes. Yes, I'll keep that in mind," she said, and slipped outside into the cool, refreshing morning air.

*Melinda!* She let the name roll over and over in her mind. Charles had cried out for Melinda in his hour of greatest need. Oh, what a fool she had been to allow herself to dwell on such impossible dreams!

## nine

"Which silk flower do you think looks best on this hat, Amy? The rose or the carnation?" Margaret held up Mrs. Crowder's almost-finished hat. "I don't want the blossom to overpower the delicate appearance of this pale pink moiré."

Amy turned her attention from the mysterious workings of the new sewing machine and gave the matter some thought. She dipped her head this way and that to study the hat from all angles. At length, she said, "Definitely the carnation. It's smaller and daintier, like Mrs. Crowder herself. I believe the carnation would be the better choice for her."

"That's what I thought too," Margaret agreed. She returned the rose to a box of assorted millinery decorations and pinned the carnation onto the narrow silk hatband. "What do you think of that?" She lifted the hat for Amy's approval.

"A little more to the left, I think," Amy said, tipping her head to one side to give a more accurate critique. "Yes, that's it. Right there," she said as Margaret repositioned the flower. "Oh, that's lovely. Mrs. Crowder is sure to be pleased."

"I hope so," Margaret said, wearily pushing back the stray lock of hair that fell across her face. "This is my last project before my trip, and I do need to get home and start packing."

Amy's heart sank. She had tried to push thoughts of Margaret's journey from her mind, hoping that by some chance she would change her mind and decide to stay. Working alongside Margaret every day helped Amy repress her thoughts of Charles, or, more specifically, of the mysterious Melinda. Left alone in the shop every day, that would be hard to do.

Of course, she was still interested in Charles's welfare. He was a good friend, but he could never be anything more. Each day she asked God to help her accept the inevitable and get on with her life.

Nevertheless, she felt a great surge of relief when Margaret reported that, after four days, Dr. Gorrie had released Charles from the hospital. Mikal had brought a carriage to take Charles home and had helped him settle back into his simple quarters behind the warehouse.

According to Margaret, Mikal had stocked his shelves with a few supplies, including three sealed jars of Margaret's nourishing soups. As soon as she heard, Amy had sent several loaves of her dark, rich, whole-wheat bread and a jar of pickled eggs.

"Mikal makes regular visits to check on him, but he absolutely forbids me to set foot inside Charles's room until he is completely well," Margaret explained. "That might take a very long time. John Gorrie stops in to see him on his daily rounds, and apparently Charles is making satisfactory progress, but Mikal says he's still awfully weak."

Amy's brow furrowed. Now that Mikal and Margaret were leaving, how would Charles manage? Perhaps she would send Alex down to check on him and see if he needed any help.

A bell jingled, and Amy stood to wait on the two customers who walked through the doorway. Her daydreams momentarily pushed aside, she stepped to the counter and forced a smile upon her face. "Good morning, ladies. Can I help you?"

❧

Charles heard a light knock on the warehouse door before Mikal pushed it ajar and stuck his head into the crack. "Anybody home? May I come in?"

Charles gave a derisive snort. "Of course I'm home. Where else would I be?" He rose from his cot and added a stick of pine to the cookstove in the corner. Seeing Mikal wipe his brow prompted him to ask, "Is it too warm in here for you?"

"No, I'm fine," Mikal said in a less-than-convincing tone.

Charles saw him eye the fire in the stove and the two quilts that lay in a heap at the foot of the bed, but he didn't try to explain how frequent chills continued to wrack his body day and night. Instead, he pushed aside a dented tin pot of cold grits—remnants of his breakfast—and offered his guest a seat at the table.

"How 'bout I make us a pot of coffee?" Mikal offered.

Charles shifted uneasily, not wanting to confess the scarcity of his supplies. "No, I, um—"

"It's okay, Friend. I brought some coffee with me." Mikal pulled a pouch from his pocket and put it on the table. He poured water from a jar into the coffeepot and placed it on the stove.

The sooty coffeepot and the dented pan had come from the galley of the *Windsong,* as had most of the room's meager furnishings. Charles wondered how he would ever be able to repay Mikal for his multitude of kindnesses.

The coffee began to gurgle with a pleasant sound, and soon the room was filled with the rich aroma of the fresh brew. Mikal poured coffee into two tin cups and stirred a spoonful of sugar into each. "Let's drink up before I have to go." He started to hand one of the cups to Charles but quickly set it back down on the table. "Ouch! These cups are hot."

Charles pushed himself up off the cot and moved to sit across the table from Mikal. He took a sip of the scalding brew and sighed. "Mm! That's good!" He held his hands in the rising steam as though to warm them.

A comfortable silence fell on the room as the two men

sipped their coffee. Charles wished he had a biscuit or at least a piece of corn bread to offer his guest.

"I'd like to stick around here and help you, my friend, but I'm expecting some cotton growers from Georgia who want to arrange a shipment on my next trip to New York."

"Cotton in April?" Charles asked, propping his elbows on the table to support his head. "I thought that was a summer crop."

"Right. But the farmers are still bringing their bales down the river—bales they've had stored in their barns all winter. I'm getting as much of it as I can on the *Windsong* to take along when I go North next week."

"And what will you be bringing back this time—besides baby clothes?" Charles asked.

"They're still cutting ice from the frozen lakes up North, and I want to bring back a load before the spring thaw. We put sawdust between the chunks of ice to keep them from sticking together, and we haul them to the icehouse here in Apalachicola. But you're right. I'm certain my wife will take steps to ensure our son has all the latest things in infant wear."

Mikal pushed himself up from the table. "I'll be back to talk to you again tomorrow, Charles. I hope you'll feel up to considering a proposal by then. You see, I need someone to take care of my record books while I'm away. I know how much you prefer working outdoors; but if you'd consider taking on this responsibility for me for a couple of months while I'm gone, it would be a great relief."

Charles raised his eyebrows and gave Mikal a skeptical look. Mikal's carefully devised plan did not fool him for a minute. He recognized that his benefactor's offer was a generous plan to keep him gainfully employed until he regained his strength. For a brief moment, his pride tried to surface, but he was in no position to protest. Instead, he nodded his head, and his anxiety lifted like a curtain. "I can do that, Mikal. I've had quite a bit of experience with record-keeping, and I promise to keep a close eye on things here while you're gone."

Mikal rose and patted him on the shoulder. "I knew I could count on you, Charles. I'll be back to discuss the details with you later. And there's one other favor I'd like to ask of you while I'm away."

"Anything I'm capable of, you know I'll try to do." There was no hesitation in Charles's reply as he met Mikal's gaze with his tired eyes.

"Well, you know my wife and I have an interest in the millinery shop—both a business interest and a personal one."

Charles sat up straighter and leaned forward to listen intently to Mikal's words. "Yes, of course."

"I'm well aware you won't be able to get out and do much of anything for awhile yet, Charles; but as the weeks go by, I'm confident your strength will return. When you feel up to it, I'd just like for you to keep an eye on the shop, to make sure there's nothing Amy needs, either for the shop or for herself."

"It would give me the greatest of pleasure to do that, Mikal. I'm already feeling stronger every day. I don't think it will be long before—"

"Please don't push yourself, Charles. Wait until John gives you the go-ahead. I'll speak to him about it before I leave; and if he says you're ready to get about, I'll be satisfied. But let's let the doctor decide." He set his cup on the table and moved to the door. "Well, I must run now, Charles. I'll stop in and see you on the morrow." With those words, he stepped out the door and into the street.

# ten

Amy's heart felt heavier than the voluminous satin gown she held draped over her lap. With small stitches, she patiently sewed a row of pearl beads around the purple edges of its pointed waistline, taking care not to prick her finger with the sharp needle. In another hour she should have the elaborate creation finished and ready to press, culminating two weeks of hard and tedious work.

If Margaret were here, the two of them would probably consider it an occasion for celebration; but with her friend and employer sailing the high seas, miles away from Apalachicola, Amy felt no enthusiasm for any kind of celebrating.

Ever since Easter, business on Market Street had slowed almost to a standstill; and Amy had again resumed the tasks of cutting her own gowns, cleaning the store, and keeping up with the few customers who straggled in. She could hardly afford to pay Rachel and Priscilla unless there was enough work to keep them busy.

But it wasn't the work Amy minded. She was used to hard work. No, it was the long hours of loneliness that plagued her. She could never get used to loneliness.

Hearing the doorbell jingle, she glanced up from her work to see Alex trudging in from school, his slate under one arm. She greeted him with a smile. "Hello, Dear. How was school today? Did you have a good day?"

Alex mumbled something and hurried up the stairs, keeping his face turned away from her. What was the matter with that boy? He usually stopped to share some of his adventures of the day, and ask what he could find to eat.

Fear gripped her heart—the same fear that ran rampant through the town. She prayed her son wasn't coming down with an illness. Over his protests, she'd been making him wear a clove of garlic in his shoes every day, and she had not been sparing in her use of vinegar. Nevertheless, Amy knew there was no sure way to prevent the dreaded disease that was sweeping the South.

She folded her work carefully and laid it aside before she followed her son upstairs. "Alex, what's wrong? Are you sick?"

"No, Ma'am," came his muffled reply. She found him lying on his cot, his face buried in his corn-husk pillow. "I–I reckon I'm just tired." He did not raise his head.

Amy's heart ached with apprehension. "Alex, sit up and let me look at you!" She reached out to place her hand on his forehead, then drew back with a gasp. "Alex! What happened to you?" She tugged at his shoulder until he sat up on the side of his cot.

The boy's eye was puffed and ringed with an angry circle of black, and he refused to meet her stern gaze. Instead he studied a square patch on his quilt and said nothing.

"Oh, Alex! You've been fighting, haven't you?"

The boy nodded to confirm her fears, still avoiding her eyes. He tried to return to his pillow, but Amy held him fast. "Who did this to you, Alex?"

Amy was perplexed by her son's silence. She had never known him to be reluctant to talk. After several unsuccessful attempts to receive an answer, she moved to the washstand and dampened a cloth with cool water. "Hold this on your eye, Alex," she commanded. "I want to get to the bottom of this."

Downstairs the bell tinkled, announcing the arrival of a customer. "Keep a cold compress on that eye until I get back," Amy called over her shoulder as she hurried down the stairs. "We'll talk more about this later."

Amy had a hard time keeping her mind on business, but she sold a gentleman two books and a magazine for his wife. As soon as she deposited the money in the cash box, she locked the front door and hurried back upstairs to see her son.

He lowered the cloth from his eye, and Amy was pleased to see that the swelling was going down. It would be some time before the color returned to normal. "Alex, I want to hear about this."

"I'm sorry, Mama. I won't fight no more, but please don't ask me 'cause I can't tell you what it was about. I just can't."

Alex had never defied her before. Amy wasn't sure how best to handle his unacceptable behavior. If only Mikal were here, she might ask his opinion. It would not be the first time she had sought his advice on matters concerning her male child. Motherhood seemed to come naturally to her, but assuming the role of father was becoming increasingly hard.

A pot of Hoppin' John simmered on the stove. She had planned to send Alex down to Mikal's waterfront warehouse with a jar of it for Charles's supper. She had never visited him there herself; but with Margaret away, she was sure a nourishing meal would be welcome. She could talk to him about Alex; and if he felt up to it, perhaps he might speak to the boy later from a man's point of view.

She dished up a hearty portion of the mixture of black-eyed peas and rice and sealed it in a glass jar. She snuggled it in her basket and added several squares of corn bread and a jar of guava jelly. On an impulse, she included a bar of the lye soap she had made last week. Although she had scented the soap with orange blossoms, perhaps Charles would not consider it too feminine for a man to use. She covered the whole thing with a napkin made from one of her calico remnants and turned to tell Alex where she would be.

She was surprised to see him sitting at the table, poring over the dictionary. "I'm glad to see you taking your lessons more seriously, Son. Can I help you find something?"

"Um, no, Ma'am." He flipped several pages and ran his finger up and down the column of words. "Mama, what's a 'wanting hussy'?"

Amy almost dropped her basket. "Alex, where did you hear that expression?" She didn't bother to tell him that he didn't have it exactly right. That was one expression he did not need to be taught.

"Um, at school. Never mind. It ain't important." He continued to peruse the dictionary under Amy's watchful stare.

She could see it was useless to pursue the subject with him. He had closed her out. Yes, she definitely needed to talk to a man about her son.

❧

Amy gathered her courage and rapped gently on the warehouse door. When it opened and she saw Charles standing there, she was momentarily at a loss for words.

"My, what a pleasant surprise!" He held the door open for her. "Come in to my humble abode."

He was terribly thin, and his cheeks had not lost their pallor, but Amy thought him the most handsome man she had ever seen. Her knees felt like wet paper that threatened to fold at any minute, and her heart pounded in her chest.

She looked right and then left, up and down the deserted street. If she understood Alex's question correctly, apparently her reputation had already been tarnished; but she didn't want to further feed the rumormongers. Yet even as she hesitated, her feet moved forward, defying all her good intentions.

Charles closed the door and led her to his only chair. He took a seat on the edge of his cot.

"I'm glad to see you up and about, Charles." She uncovered her basket and placed the food on his table. She hoped he wouldn't notice the tremor in her hands.

A wide smile covered his face. "Yes, I'm feeling much

stronger. I've been getting out a little each day, trying to keep an eye on Mikal's properties while he's away." He stretched his long legs out in front of him and crossed them at the ankles. "Now tell me how things are going at your place. I'm supposed to keep a watch on that too, you know."

"Oh, no. I didn't know. I wouldn't want to add to your burdens; and besides, I'm getting along just fine."

He gave her a probing look. "Are you, Amy? Are you really fine?"

Did this man have an uncanny ability to read her mind, or was her concern for Alex etched in her face? "I should have said 'the shop is fine,' because I do have a bit of a personal problem. I wondered if you might advise me."

Charles uncrossed his legs and leaned forward. His nearness unnerved her, but she swallowed hard and continued. "It's Alex," she said. "He came home from school today with a black eye, and he refuses to discuss it with me." She couldn't bring herself to repeat the phrase for which her son had searched the dictionary. Charles would have to ferret that information from Alex on his own.

She detected a hint of a smile forming on Charles's lips, which he quickly concealed with an artificial cough. "Amy, I know how this must concern you, but let me tell you that few boys go through life without a fight. I'm not condoning it, you understand; but I'm sure once you get the matter out in the open, you'll be able to give him wise and proper counseling."

Without thinking, Amy reached out and gripped his arm. "But don't you see? That's the problem, Charles. He won't talk to me about it." Touching his flesh sent a tingling sensation through her body, and she quickly pulled her hand away. "I just thought perhaps you could speak to him about it—to find out if there's a problem I need to know about. I think he might be more willing to talk to a man about it."

"I'll certainly try, Amy. I see Alex almost every morning

when he sells his newspapers along the waterfront. I'll make it a point to talk to the lad tomorrow."

Amy stood and drew her shawl around her shoulders. "I must be going, then. I don't like to trouble you, but if you—"

Charles stood to face her. "I assure you it's never any trouble to do something to help you, Amy. You're the kindest, loveliest lady I've ever known." He took a step closer to her and held her arms with his big hands. As their eyes locked, time seemed to stand still for both of them, until. . .

A sharp knock sounded on the door, and without waiting for an answer, John Gorrie stepped into the room. "Well, well. I see you're feeling much better, Charles." A smile played on his lips. "I didn't mean to interrupt anything."

Amy's cheeks felt like hot coals. She was sure her face was bright scarlet. "I—I just dropped by to bring a basket of food for Charles. I was already on my way out." She picked up her empty basket and slid past them toward the door.

"Wait, Amy," Charles protested. "I didn't even thank you properly for bringing my supper. I know it will be delicious. And I'll give some thought to what we talked about."

He continued to call after her, but his words were lost in the wind as she hurried through the doorway and down the street. What must John think of her? Or even more important, what would have happened had John not arrived when he did? Indeed, she *was* acting like a wanton hussy. She had to get a grip on herself and start acting like a respectable matron should.

## eleven

Phlox in various tones of pink and white grew in wild profusion along the streets of Apalachicola, peppering the ground with their colorful blooms. The sweet scent of magnolia blossoms drifted on the crisp spring breeze.

With her market basket over her arm, Amy walked briskly down the sidewalk toward the general store. She needed a nice, meaty bone and a few fresh vegetables for her soup pot. Her own garden was coming along nicely, but she wanted a parsnip or two and some celery, neither of which grew in her small backyard plot.

Approaching the general store, she saw two of her best customers coming through the door. Amy held up her skirt as she climbed the front steps. "Good morning, ladies," she called cordially.

"Hmph!" Both ladies turned their faces to the side and ignored her completely. Could it be that, under the shade of her sunbonnet, they had both failed to recognize her? She was tempted to call after them, but they scurried away so fast that there was no chance for conversation.

Inside the store, only kind Mr. Diamanti spoke to her. His customers all seemed to be unusually busy concentrating on their selections and either didn't see Amy or chose to ignore her.

She made her selections at the meat counter: a beef shoulder bone and a slab of salt pork for her beans. "I'd like a pound of those pinto beans," she said, pointing to a large wooden barrel. Mr. Diamanti used a big silver scoop to measure out the beans and weigh them on his scales. "What else can I get for you today, Mrs. McCutcheon?" His eyes darted nervously around the room. "How 'bout one of these here cabbages? Just cut this morning. Nice and fresh."

"No, thank you, Mr. Diamanti. I think I have what I need." Amy pulled a few coins out of her reticule and handed them to the storekeeper. "If you need Alex to run any deliveries for you, tomorrow's Saturday, and he'll be available all day."

"Well, um, that's good to know, Mrs. McCutcheon. Seems as how most of my customers been coming in and carrying out their groceries themselves lately, but I'll keep Alex in mind."

Amy was beginning to read a picture here, and it wasn't pretty. Was the whole town intent on snubbing her—and her son, as well? She had done nothing to be ashamed of. Was it because she had helped Charles Drake when he was sick, or could it be due to some vicious tales circulated by the vindictive Mrs. Simpson? These were the same women she saw in church every Sunday; the ones who raised their voices in the verses of "A Charge to Keep I Have" and "God Is Love; His Mercy Brightens."

Several women clustered in the corner, casting furtive glances in her direction. Amy didn't have time for idle gossip, either to listen or participate. She picked up her packages and left the store, her head held high.

As she walked out into the late afternoon sunshine, she was surprised to see Charles crossing the street in her direction. He looked so much stronger, and his face bore a healthy glow that had been missing the last time she saw him.

"Amy! What a great piece of luck that I should run into you. I planned to stop by your shop and return these jars." He indicated the burlap bag he carried. "How can I ever repay you for all your kindness?"

"What little help I was able to offer wasn't meant to be a debt, Charles." Amy saw from the corner of her eye that the group of gossiping women had moved to the porch and were keeping a close watch on the two of them. She refused to be intimidated by them. "I'm afraid I can't carry anything else just now because my basket is full of groceries; but if you have time to come by the shop, I'll make a pot of tea."

The familiar smile she had secretly grown to love spread across his clean-shaven face. "I'd be honored to have tea with you, Mrs. McCutcheon." He spoke in a voice loud enough to be heard by the curious bystanders. "I think all the citizens of Apalachicola could learn a valuable lesson from you about making a newcomer feel welcome. You are a very gracious woman."

Amy blushed. Was he deliberately putting on a show for the ladies? She shifted her gaze and watched the little group disperse and go in opposite directions, but it would only be a matter of time before they met again to damage a good name—either hers or someone else's. She thought it sad that their lives didn't have more interesting activities.

"You're looking much better these days, Charles," Amy said as he kept in step beside her. "Is John still stopping in to see you every day?"

"Not every day, but several times a week. I wish he wouldn't. I don't feel the need of a doctor's care any longer, and I already owe him more than I'm able to pay."

Dust swirled up around their shoes as they walked along the unpaved street. The western sky had turned a rosy orange as the sun dipped toward the horizon. Glass jars rattled in the burlap sack Charles carried in one hand, while he used his other hand to carry Amy's grocery basket.

"Will Alex be home when we get there?" Charles asked her.

Amy shook her head. "Probably not. He often goes down to the waterfront after school, hoping to pick up some extra change by running errands. Why? Did you need to see him?" She looked anxiously up into his face, wondering if Alex had gotten himself into any more trouble she didn't know about.

Charles chuckled. "No, actually I was hoping he'd be out somewhere so I could talk to you privately about him."

Amy's heart lurched in apprehension, but she kept her fears to herself.

When they arrived at the millinery shop, Amy extracted a big skeleton key from her reticule to unlock the front door. "Come in, Charles. I'll put the kettle on, and then I'd like to hear whatever it is you have to say about my son."

She offered Charles a chair before she ran upstairs to make the tea on her cookstove. "I'll be right back."

She was glad she had made some raisin scones before opening the shop that morning. She put them on a plate and got down two of her porcelain teacups. When the water boiled, she steeped the tea and poured it into the cups. She took her sugar bowl down from the shelf and sliced a lemon from a bowl of fruit on the table. At last she was ready to serve her guest.

Balancing the tray in both hands, she teetered on the steps, and Charles jumped up to meet her halfway and help her. "Mm! Scones! I haven't had those since Mel—since I came to Apalachicola."

Amy pretended not to notice his slip of the tongue, though she knew very well what he had almost said. *He hadn't had scones since Melinda made them for him!* Someday she would ask him about Melinda but not until she knew him much better than she did now. "What was it you wanted to tell me about Alex, Charles?"

Charles's hands looked massive as he gripped the dainty cup handle between his fingers. He took a sip of tea before he answered her. "Well, I talked to him like you asked. Did he tell you about that?"

"No, he didn't." Amy was surprised. She wondered why Alex would not have mentioned such an important conversation. She found Alex coming to her less often with his problems. With a mixture of pride and sorrow, Amy was fast beginning to realize that her son was no longer "Mama's little boy." Before she knew it, he would be a man. Sometimes the enormity of the responsibility scared her. "Were you able to convince him that his ungentlemanly behavior was unacceptable?"

Charles chuckled until his shoulders shook. Then suddenly sobering, he set his teacup on a sewing table and leaned forward to look deep into her eyes. The soft tenderness in his voice was akin to a caress. "Amy, do you have any idea what your son was fighting about?"

Amy felt warm color rising to her face. Was it caused by the endearing tone Charles had used, or was it because she actually did have a vague idea as to what prompted the fight? She wasn't sure she wanted to talk to Charles about that. Instead, she said, "Do you know who hit him?"

Now Charles guffawed. He couldn't begin to control his laughter. Amy was not amused. "I hardly see the humor in this very serious situation," she said.

"I'm sorry," he apologized, still trying to control his emotions. "But you might laugh too when you hear who gave him that shiner."

"Oh, I can just imagine," Amy wailed. "It was probably that mean Jimmy Jones. He's twice the size of Alex and two years older. He's such a bully. It was Jimmy, wasn't it?"

Though he tried hard to maintain a straight face, Amy could see Charles's shoulders begin to jiggle again. "No," he said. "It wasn't Jimmy."

"Who then?" Amy's curiosity was piqued. What brute had taken unfair advantage of her little boy?

"I don't think he wants me to tell anyone because he's pretty embarrassed by it, Amy, but he got socked in the eye by some little girl named Mattilou."

"Mattilou!" Amy was on her feet. "Why, that's impossible. She's just a little girl."

"I'm sorry, Amy." Again Charles had to apologize for a fit of laughter. "That's why he didn't want to tell anyone. He's so embarrassed that a girl could get the best of him."

"But why, Charles? Why would Mattilou even *want* to hit Alex?"

"Well, er. . ." This time it was Charles's turn to be embarrassed. "It seems this little girl—this Mattilou—repeated some malicious gossip she had learned from her mother about, um, about someone Alex cares about, and he tried to defend her name."

Just as she had suspected. Alex had fought to protect her reputation. "Are you saying he hit Mattilou first?" This story seemed to grow worse and worse by the minute.

"No, of course he wouldn't hit a girl. That's what made it so hard for him. He said he could have defended himself against another boy, but a girl, well. . .he decided under the circumstances it might be permissible to give her a gentle shove." Here again, Charles fought the insistent smile that tugged at his lips. "Just a little ladylike push, you understand, and then the kid hauled off and punched him in the eye. Because she was a girl, he couldn't retaliate, and now he's taking a lot of teasing from the boys at school."

Amy covered her face with her hands. "Oh, Charles, whatever am I going to do? I hardly know how to talk to him anymore. I want so much to teach him proper behavior. I take him to church every week, and we read the Bible together, but. . ." Here her voice trailed off. Did Charles realize the importance of the Bible in a young boy's life?

He seemed to read her thoughts. "You are certainly to be commended for that, Amy. 'Train up a child in the way he should go: and when he is old, he will not depart from it.' That's what it says in Proverbs, and I believe it, don't you?"

"Yes. Oh, yes. Charles, this is not the first time I've heard you quote Scripture. So may I assume you are a Christian, then?"

Charles hesitated. He ran a hand through his sandy hair. "Let's just say I'm a backslider, and let it go at that." He picked up his teacup. "Anyway, I believe we were talking about your son." He shifted in his chair, and Amy could detect his discomfort, but she had wondered about this too long to let it go. This seemed the perfect time to get some answers.

"I'd like to understand what you mean by 'backslider.' Either you belong to Christ or you don't, and it's important to me to know which." There. She'd said it. Admitted to Charles that he was important to her. If she was to be humiliated by her admission, then so be it.

"What a very special lady you are, Amy." He leaned forward and looked tenderly into her somber eyes. "I am so touched by your concern. You can't imagine how much it means to me. I've been struggling to refrain from admitting what you've come to mean to me, but now that you've given me a small ray of hope—"

His eyes seemed to probe the depths of her heart, and she was sure he must be able to hear its thunder. She lowered her gaze to break the intensity. But as quickly as she had allowed her emotions to rise to the surface, an alarm went off in her mind, and she fought to suppress them. She clasped her hands and folded them demurely in her lap. Were his words simply a way of changing the subject? And what about Melinda? She still had too many unanswered questions where Charles Drake was concerned.

"We were not talking about you and me, Charles. What I asked about was your spiritual life and whether or not you are a Christian. You've told me so very little about yourself that I feel I hardly know you. I–I treasure your friendship, Charles, but I didn't mean for my words to stimulate your hope for anything beyond that."

Charles looked as though he had received a splash of cold water in his face. "I understand, Amy. I'm sorry if I spoke out of turn. And yes, I admit I've been evasive with you about my personal life. I've had my reasons for that. But if it's details you want, then details you shall have. I must warn you, though, they won't be pretty."

# twelve

A myriad of questions had tormented Amy ever since the day she first met Charles Drake right here in the millinery shop. Now, just when he seemed ready to unveil some crucial answers, their conversation was interrupted by the arrival of Alex.

Her son came bouncing through the door yelling, "What's for supper, Mama? I'm starving." Then catching sight of Charles, he halted in his tracks and pulled the cap from his head. "Hello, Mr. Drake. 'Scuse me. I didn't know you was here."

"No reason you would, Alex, since I don't have a horse outside tied to the hitching post. Anyway, I need to be getting out of the way so you and your mama can have your supper." He stood up and pushed back his chair, shifting his attention back to Amy. "Thank you for the tea and scones. It's been a long time since I've enjoyed anything so much."

Amy's heart plummeted. Would she ever know the answers to her questions? She offered her hand in a gesture of farewell, and Charles grasped it and held tight. "We'll finish our conversation one day soon, Amy. Perhaps tomorrow, if you have the time."

Amy pulled her hand free. Time was not the problem. She would make sure she found time. The problem was the place. Where could they meet to talk in privacy without fanning the local fires of malicious gossip? "We'll just have to see how it all works out, Charles. Alex, run upstairs and bring down a jar of my apple butter for Mr. Drake. He can take it home with him when he leaves."

"Yes'm." Alex took the steps two at a time. "Be right back."

Charles moved toward the door. "I promise to come to see you again soon, Amy," he repeated as soon as Alex disappeared up the stairs. "I'll try to tell you all the things you want to know. In the meantime, try not to judge me too harshly until you hear my story. After that, I'll just have to let you make up your own mind about me."

Footsteps bounded down the stairs. "Here it is, Mr. Drake," Alex said, extending a jar of apple butter. "This is real good stuff. My mama makes the best apple butter of anybody in the whole Florida Territory."

"I'm sure she does," Charles agreed. Gripping the jar in one hand and the doorknob in the other, he shifted his gaze back to Amy. "Thank you again for everything. You've managed to turn an ordinary afternoon into one of indescribable pleasure." With a wink of his eye, he opened the door and slipped out into the twilight.

❧

Charles kicked fiercely at the pebbles scattered along the street, trying to vent his frustrations as he walked south toward the waterfront. His heart was heavy with the choices that confronted him.

Of course Amy wanted some answers. She had a right to know about his life before he came to Apalachicola. But how would she feel about him once she heard his story?

He hadn't come to the Gulf Coast to pursue emotional entanglements. On the contrary, he had hoped to settle a few problems that already complicated his life, a life that seemed so sweet and simple just a year ago. Could his life ever be uncomplicated again?

He lifted his eyes to the heavens, where the first stars of the evening were beginning to twinkle against a background of cobalt blue, reminding him again of the vastness of God's universe. If only he could reconnect and take his problems to the Lord, the way he had always done for most of his life.

He had tried so many times before, but he always got bogged down when he came to the part about forgiving those who trespassed against him. How could God expect him to forgive those men who had come in the dead of night and robbed him of everything he held most dear, including his precious mother?

He had tried to purge his mind of vengeance, to concentrate on building a new life for himself in a new land. And he might have been able to do that—but for Melinda. Always Melinda. She was never far from his thoughts. He had promised to return to her, and return he would, as soon as he could earn enough money to help them both start anew.

He quickened his steps with a new resolve. He would find a time and a place to talk to Amy, and he would lay out his life story, just as he had promised. Whatever feelings she might have for him after that might be painful to bear, but at least it would be built on a foundation of truth.

Amy had made it perfectly clear today that friendship was all he could ever expect from her. That was only a fragile cord of what he might have hoped for, but even that tender thread was precious to him. He fervently hoped it would not be severed by the truth she would hear.

# thirteen

Alex hurried down the road to the one-room schoolhouse where Miss Slade held a daily class for fourteen children of assorted ages. Alex hated school. He couldn't understand why his mama thought it was so important.

He already knew how to read, and he could cipher as long as the numbers weren't too big. This week it seemed like Japan was all Miss Slade could talk about. Why in the world did he need to learn about people he would never know and who couldn't talk with him even if he went there to meet them? He would much rather be doing something useful, like selling newspapers, or shining shoes, or delivering groceries to the ladies of Apalachicola.

He carried his noon meal in a galvanized pail. His mama always insisted on sending what she called nourishing food and checked when he returned home to make sure he had eaten it all. Dinnertime was embarrassing to Alex because most of his friends just brought cold biscuits or corn bread. Some of the girls seemed to carry an endless supply of sweets, the kind his mama said might ruin his teeth.

He was already late, so a few more minutes couldn't make much difference. He veered off his path to a clear stream that branched off from the Apalachicola River. He'd have a cool drink of water beneath the trees and then be on his way.

As he approached the creek, he heard an unfamiliar noise. It sounded like someone crying. Alex quickened his step; and rounding a big cypress tree, he saw a little girl sitting on a rock by the stream, her face buried in her hands. At first he couldn't tell who she was; but when he drew closer, he saw that it was his nemesis, Mattilou Simpson!

His first impulse was to run; but in spite of the bad feelings between the two of them, her wracking sobs touched a part of his young heart. "Mattilou? What's the matter?"

"Go away," she said between sobs. Still she did not raise her eyes.

Alex took two steps to close the gap that separated them. "Are you hurt? Why are you crying?"

Mattilou stood up and wiped her cheeks with her hands. "I'm not crying. I–I just have a cold. Go mind your own business, Alex McCutcheon. Just leave me alone."

Realizing he held the upper hand emboldened Alex, so he said, "Not until you tell me what's the matter. I'm staying here until you tell me."

Mattilou slumped back down on the rock. "A lot you'd care. I was on my way to school, and I tripped over a limb the wind blew down in the road, and I fell down."

"So you're hurt, then. Did you sprain your ankle or what?"

"I already told you I'm not hurt!" Mattilou screamed. Then she softened her voice. "I got dirt on my pinafore. Mama's going to be furious. And besides that, the latch on my dinner pail came open and all my dinner landed in the mud. Now I don't have anything to eat, so I can't go to school." She again began to wail into her hands.

"Aw, Mattilou, grow up and quit acting like a baby. Here, hand me your pinafore and I'll wash the mud off in the creek. It'll be dry before you get to school."

Mattilou was so surprised by his words that she quit crying and looked at him. Then, as one accustomed to obeying commands, she slipped her muslin pinafore off her shoulders and handed it to Alex. The calico dress she wore beneath it bore no traces of dirt.

Alex stepped on stones to reach the middle of the creek,

teetering precariously as the water rushed by. Then he bent and swished the garment in the stream, rubbing the offending spot just as he had seen his mother do every wash day. He twisted the water out of the pinafore and held it up for her to see. "Look, Mattilou. It's clean as a whistle."

"Be careful you don't slip," she cautioned as he made his way back to the bank. Alex was surprised. Any other time, she would have been hoping to see him fall into the creek and douse his own clothes. It was the first time he could ever remember hearing her say anything nice to him.

Alex hung her pinafore over a tree branch. "It won't take it long to dry in this wind." Then he picked up her dinner pail and rinsed it off in the edge of the stream. "Now, about your food," he said. He found he rather liked taking charge of things. He lifted the lid of his own bucket and began to share its contents.

"Oh, no! You mustn't give me your dinner. What will you eat?"

"There's more than enough here," he assured her, pulling out pickled eggs, oranges, cold chicken, corn bread slathered with apple butter, and molasses cookies for dessert. "Look, my mama even put in an extra napkin. She musta known I'd be sharing today."

Mattilou looked contrite. "Alex, I–I'm sorry about the time I hit you. I shouldn't have done that."

Alex blushed at the mention of that embarrassing day. "Aw, that was nothin', Mattilou. I didn't hardly feel it at all. But if you're gonna learn to fight, you need to—"

"But I'm *not*, Alex. I'm never going to do that again. My mother said it was most unladylike for a girl to fight. I just wanted you to know I'm sorry."

"Well, I reckon I had it comin' to me, Mattilou. I know I shouldn't call anybody bad names, and I shouldn't push girls neither, even if they say things about my mother that aren't true."

Mattilou bit her bottom lip. "I shouldn't have said mean

things about your mother, Alex. Miss Amy has always been nice to me. I guess I was just mad that day, and I apologize."

Alex squirmed uncomfortably, anxious to change the subject. "Say, while we're waiting for your dress to dry, we might as well go ahead and eat, because it'll be past noon by the time we get to the schoolhouse."

When Mattilou didn't object to his suggestion, he took the two gingham napkins and spread them out on the ground. Mattilou helped arrange the food on them, and Alex said the blessing.

Alex looked over his shoulder, first to the right and then to the left. What would his friends think if they could see him now, sitting here in the cool shade by the creek, enjoying a picnic lunch with Mattilou Simpson? But did it really matter what they might think? He looked at Mattilou and grinned broadly before he popped a whole egg in his mouth at once. He was mighty hungry.

⋙

Amy tried to keep her mind focused on her work during the days following her visit from Charles. He had promised to talk to her, to answer the questions that had plagued her since their very first meeting. Who was Charles Drake? Where was he from? Why had he come to Apalachicola? And most important of all, why had he hardened his heart against God? She longed to ask him all this and more, but he hadn't made any attempt to contact her. The next move would be up to him. She certainly couldn't pursue him like a. . .a. . .*wanton hussy!*

The weather had turned warm and balmy after Easter, and the gentry of Apalachicola began to prepare for the hot months ahead. Amy unfurled bolts of dimity and silk, organdy and lace, to be viewed and fingered by style-conscious women. The pages of her *Godey's Lady's Book* became wrinkled and dog-eared from almost constant use. She sketched and planned dresses, bonnets, and parasols for summer, all the while wondering how and when she and Charles might have a chance for their private talk.

At least one of her trials seemed to be easing. For the past week, Alex had not uttered a single complaint about getting to school on time, and he had even washed his face and combed his hair without her daily reminder. Surely her son must be growing up!

Amy was counting out change to the lady who had just purchased a copy of *Saturday Evening Post* when the bell over the door jingled and a flurry of excited voices rose like a flock of starlings. She looked up and silently thanked God. Margaret had returned! The customers crowded around her like ants at a picnic so that Amy could only stand back and wait her turn.

At last Margaret pushed her way through the store to circle the counter and embrace Amy in a warm, tight hug. "Oh, it's so good to see you again!"

Amy gripped her friend's arms and held her out for inspection, smiling at the recognizable swelling beneath Margaret's skirts. "You look wonderful, Margaret. I can already see that motherhood is going to agree with you."

"Oh, yes! I can't wait to show you all the things I've brought back for our baby. I bought yarn too, and I'm learning to knit. Will you help me, Amy?"

"Of course," Amy assured her, giving her an extra hug. Amy hoped Margaret had brought back more than baby clothes. She wanted to hear all about the latest New York fashions, but this was probably not the best time to mention it.

The customers forgot about clothing for the moment, eager to hear details of Margaret's journey. "When did you get back?" "Where is that handsome husband of yours?" "Did the sea make you nauseous?" The questions came faster than Margaret could answer them.

While all this was going on, Amy slipped quietly upstairs to put a kettle of water on the stove for tea. She had plenty of questions of her own for Margaret, and she hoped the two of them could find a moment for private conversation before long.

By late morning the excitement had died down, and once again the women were perusing the catalogues for new ideas for summer dresses and hats. Margaret whispered an aside to Amy. "Let's hang the sign on the door and lock up during the noon hour."

Amy didn't need any urging. She hung the sign and waited for the last two ladies to leave. "Now," she said, clapping her hands in anticipation, "let's go upstairs and have our tea. I made some scones this morning; I'll open some of my apple-sauce to go with them."

"Mm! That sounds wonderful. I declare, I must be eating for at least three. I seem to stay hungry all the time."

Amy laughed, and Margaret followed her up the stairs to the familiar room where she herself had once lived.

Seated at the small oak table, the two women exchanged information of the happenings of the last couple of months while sipping sassafras tea and munching on their sweets. The minutes flew by until at last they could hear impatient knocks on their storefront door.

"You've only been home for less than a day, Margaret. You must be very tired." Amy placed a net cover over the food and brushed the crumbs from the table. "I'll handle the customers this afternoon, but I'd be happy for your help tomorrow."

Margaret stood and stretched, placing the palms of her hands against her lower back. "I am a bit drowsy," she admitted. "But I'll be here to work early tomorrow. I'll bring my knitting too, just in case we have a few moments to call our own." She kissed her friend on the cheek, and Amy went downstairs to respond to the demands of their customers.

# fourteen

Charles Drake waited until dusk to walk across town to the millinery shop on Market Street. He didn't care who knew about his strong feelings for Amy McCutcheon; but he'd heard about the local gossipmongers, and the last thing on earth he wanted to do was cause Amy any embarrassment.

He was relieved to see the glow of a candle through her downstairs window. He picked up his pace and hurried toward her porch.

A soft knock brought her to the door. Charles felt his heart skip a beat when he heard first her footsteps crossing the floor and then a click as she turned the latch.

"Yes?" A small crack of light slid through the narrow opening, but Amy warily kept a firm hold on the door until she identified her visitor. "Oh, Charles!" Her hands flew to her hair, and she tried frantically to tuck stray ringlets from her forehead into her braid. She hesitated for just a moment before opening the door wide and inviting him in.

"I–I was just sweeping up down here, getting ready for the morrow. Alex is upstairs doing his homework. We've. . .we've just finished our supper." She babbled on nervously, backing her way into the room as Charles followed.

"I apologize for coming unannounced," he began. "I know you weren't expecting me tonight, Amy. If this is inconvenient for you, I can come another time. But the fact is, we do need to talk."

"Yes. Yes, we do." Amy met his gaze and nodded, her dark eyes sparkling in the golden glow of candlelight. She was so incredibly beautiful. Charles yearned to reach out and touch her, to hold her close, yet he knew he had no right. She was like a lovely star that seemed so near yet was really so very far away.

He shuffled his feet, shifting his weight from left to right, waiting for an invitation to sit down; but hearing none, he suggested, "Would you like to go for a walk? It's pleasant enough outdoors if you wear a light wrap."

Amy blinked, seeming to bring her thoughts into focus. "Yes, I–I think that would be nice. Excuse me for a moment, Charles, while I run upstairs and tell Alex I'll be gone. I'll get my shawl and be back down in just a minute."

Amy gave him a fleeting smile before she disappeared up the dark stairwell. Charles cherished that smile, but what would she think of him after she heard his story? Would she smile at him still?

ﻝ

When the night air hit her, Amy pulled her shawl tighter around her shoulders. In spite of the evening chill, just as Charles had said, it was really quite pleasant out. The half-moon cast a gentle light on the quiet streets of Apalachicola, and the soft wind carried refreshing scents of the salty sea. Amy inhaled deeply, wondering what she would learn before this night ended.

She had been so eager to learn more about Charles Drake; but now that the moment of truth drew near, she wondered why she hadn't been content to let well enough alone. He was a good friend, and she should be grateful for that. He could never be more because his heart belonged to another. Somewhere in the infamous red hills to the north, Melinda waited for him to come home. The thought caused her to shiver.

"Are you cold?" he asked. "Perhaps we should turn back."

"No, I'm fine."

Charles offered his arm, and after only a moment's hesitation, Amy let her small hand rest gently in the bend of his elbow. Even through the sleeve of his coarse homespun shirt, she felt a tingling surge of warmth.

They turned on Chestnut Street and walked past Trinity Church, where Margaret and Mikal had spoken their wedding vows nearly three years ago. Amy never ceased to thrill at the sight of the massive Greek Revival structure. "Has anyone told you how this church was built?" she asked, pausing to lift her eyes toward the magnificent spires.

"Yes, Mikal told me it was John Gorrie's dream and that it was built elsewhere and brought to Apalachicola by schooner."

"Yes, John had seen a similar structure in New York. This one was actually made in New York too; but because of its size, it had to be brought to Apalachicola in sections. It took four trips by schooner before the entire structure finally came together. Many people doubted it could be done, but I choose to think of it as another one of God's miracles." When Charles didn't respond, she added, "The services there are as beautiful as the building. Has anyone ever invited you to attend?"

"Yes, Mikal has mentioned it several times, but I. . ." He pulled her forward and resumed their walk without finishing his sentence.

"Charles, this is one of the things we need to talk about. I didn't understand what you meant when you said you were a backslider. Either you've given your heart to Christ or you haven't, and please don't give me another trite response, because your answer is very important to me." Of all the things she wanted to know about him, this was the most important.

He took his time in answering. They had stopped walking again, and Charles pulled her over to a stone bench beneath a gigantic magnolia tree. The scent of the beautiful white blossoms sweetened the night air. "Amy, let's sit down here for a moment."

Amy did as he suggested, and Charles eased himself down

beside her. "Amy, I'm flattered you care so much about my relationship with God, and I'll try to tell you as straight as I can; but the truth is, I don't really know the answer myself. Yes, I gave my heart to Christ once, but I know He's closed the door on me by now."

Amy gasped. "Charles! How can you say such a thing? He would never do that! The Bible says He stands at the door and knocks. Jesus loves you, and He wants you for His own. Surely you've read enough Scripture to understand that."

"It's not that simple, Amy. I keep trying to reconnect with Him; but every time I pray the prayer that He taught us, I get bogged down in the line that says I need to forgive those who trespass against me. The simple truth of the matter is that I don't, and I know I never will. I've tried, but I can't forgive the men who robbed me of everything I held most dear."

Amy heard the crack in his voice as he spoke and knew he was very close to tears. She spoke softly, gently. "Do you want to tell me about it, Charles? If you'd rather not, it's all right. I promise not to ask you again."

He turned to face her, never letting go of her hand. "Yes, Amy. I want to tell you about it." He took a deep breath before he continued. "Just a year ago, I was a happy, hard-working rancher in the red hills. I'm sure you've heard tales about thieves and rustlers and even renegade Indians who frequent that territory, but there are a lot of good people who live there too. I had a home, cattle, horses—everything a man could ever want. And I had Christ in my heart too.

"Every Sunday I loaded up my wagon and took my mother, my sister, and some of our neighbors to the little church where I first gave my heart to the Lord. We were a happy bunch; and although we knew we lived in a place where danger surrounded us daily, we didn't dwell on it beyond taking every reasonable precaution. Yes, I kept a gun;

and although I don't consider myself a violent man, I knew how to use it."

Here he paused, and Amy could read the pain in his eyes. "You don't have to do this, Charles."

As though she hadn't spoken, Charles continued. "It happened in the dead of night. A band of outlaws set fire to our house and barn before I had any chance to respond. I guess I blame myself for that, in a way; but I'm only one man, and I couldn't stand guard day and night. My first concern, of course, was to get my mother and sister out of the house and save them from the fire, and only then did I try to go after the marauders."

He broke down and sobbed. "But I was too late. By the light of the moon, I could see their faces, and I recognized them as the notorious Washburn gang. Their pictures are posted throughout the territory: Wanted: Dead or Alive. It was easy to identify the leader, a man with an ugly purple scar on his face. I grabbed my gun and tried to follow them, but they had stolen all my horses; my cattle too. In my heart, I'm a murderer, Amy, because I would surely have killed them all if I could have."

Amy felt as though her heart would break for him. She gripped his forearm. "Enough, Charles. You've told me enough for now."

Charles lifted his head and used a bandana to wipe his face. "No, let me tell you the rest, and then maybe you'll understand why I carry such a load of vengeance in my heart.

"All three of us suffered severe burns, but my mother the worst. Her hair had caught fire, and her face was charred beyond recognition. Even so, we could have survived all this and healed in time. Neighbors saw the smoke and came running to help. But just hours after the attack, my saintly mother began to have severe chest pains. In spite of everything we tried to do for her, she passed away before dawn."

"Oh, Charles. I am so sorry." Amy's cheeks were wet with her own tears, but she let him continue.

"I nearly went crazy with grief and anger. Our neighbors took us in because we had nothing left. After we buried my mother, I vowed to find those scoundrels and bring them to justice. And I promised my sister I'd somehow earn enough money to return to the red hills and rebuild our home. I hope Melinda hasn't given up on me, though, because I intend to keep that promise, no matter how long it takes."

A spark ignited an explosion in her heart. Suddenly Amy felt weak and light-headed. Had she misunderstood the words she had just heard? "Melinda? Melinda is your *sister*?" One of the questions she'd carried was already answered without even being asked.

Charles's emotions made him oblivious to Amy's extreme reaction, or perhaps he simply attributed it to her sympathetic nature. "Yes, Melinda is all I have left of family now, and I can't let her down. That's why I came to Apalachicola. I heard work was plentiful on the Gulf Coast. Because the outlaws stole all my horses, I had to walk almost forty miles to get here. I was exhausted and near starving when you were kind enough to give me something to eat, Amy. And thanks to the kind heart of Mikal Lee, I'm now gainfully employed; but it's going to take a long time before I can save enough money to rebuild my home. Besides, with all my livestock gone, I'd have nothing to sustain us even if I did manage to build a house back there on our land."

Amy's heart began to race, and wild ideas ran through her mind. "Where is Melinda now? Can't you bring her here?"

"Amy, my sister is only twelve years old. I left her in the care of kind neighbors who assured me she'd be well taken care of for as long as she wants to stay, but she expects me to come back and make a home for her in the red hills like I promised. I have no place for her here, and she's lost so much already. I don't want to uproot her anymore."

Amy could understand his desolation, and she turned to the only source from which she knew to draw comfort. She held his hands and looked into his tear-streaked face. "Charles, let me pray for you. God will help you through this."

Charles pulled his hands free and turned his face away. "Amy, you still don't understand, do you? God doesn't care about me anymore. If He did, He'd have protected us from those savages who wrecked our lives. And like I told you, I can never forgive those men. Never!" Seeing Amy's crest-fallen face, he added, "I'm sorry, Amy. I shouldn't have burdened you with my problems, but you wanted to know. And now that you know, I can only hope you won't hate me for my weaknesses."

"Hate you? Why, Charles, I lo—I'm very fond of you. I could never hate you." Amy was grateful for the dark that hid her burning cheeks. In a moment of weakness, she had almost made a startling confession. Did she really love Charles Drake? She wasn't sure if what she felt for him was what women referred to as "falling in love." She had no experience with which to compare it. She only knew that the thought of being separated from him for the rest of her life seemed unbearable.

Charles stood and pulled her to her feet. He straightened her shawl and drew it snugly around her shoulders. Then with his big hands gripping her small ones, he lifted her slender fingers to his face and gently brushed them with his lips. Though the act was completed in only a few seconds, Amy could feel the tingling sensation traveling down to the tips of her toes. She was sorry when Charles ended the magnificent moment by raising his head and once again offering her his arm. "The wind is picking up, Amy. I need to take you home. But thank you for hearing me out tonight. And thank you for not hating me."

They walked in silence until they stood on the porch in

front of her door. "Charles, thank you for trusting me with your life story. And in spite of what you've said, I'm going to be praying for you, because the Bible promises that with God all things are possible."

She unlocked her door, and as she left him standing on the porch, she heard him whisper, "Good night, my darling. Sleep well."

# fifteen

Alex was up at first light and off to sell his papers. Amy set a pan of water on the cookstove to boil for his oatmeal. He'd be back in an hour or two, grabbing a quick breakfast before dashing off to school.

Amy dressed quickly in the chill of early morning. Lately her customers seemed to be arriving at the shop earlier and earlier, and Margaret would probably not come in to help her until midmorning.

Amy didn't mind being busy. Work kept her mind occupied and didn't let her dwell on the events that hung heavy on her mind.

Last night was certainly such an event. Learning that Melinda was Charles's sister had lifted one concern but replaced it immediately with another. One day Charles would be leaving Apalachicola to make his home in the red hills again. Of course it would likely be a long time before he attained his goal, but that was little consolation to Amy as she tried to imagine a life without Charles.

How had she allowed herself to fall in love with someone who didn't have a close relationship to the Lord? Yes, she might as well admit it to herself. She did love Charles Drake; and no matter what happened, she knew in her heart she always would. If she had wondered before, his kiss last night dispelled any lingering doubts. She touched her fingertips with her lips, remembering the sweetness of his kiss.

She had stayed awake long into the night, praying that God would somehow open Charles's heart to His love. And she'd asked God to use her as an instrument to rekindle the relationship Charles had known with the Lord before the terrible fire.

After she straightened the quilts on the two cots and slipped into her calico dress, she sat down at the table and gave thanks before eating a quick breakfast of cold corn bread covered with buttermilk. She used some of the hot water from the pan on the stove to make herself a cup of brisk tea. As soon as she stirred oatmeal into the pan and pushed it to the back of the stove to stay warm for Alex, she'd be ready to face a new day.

Her first customers arrived early to select pieces from the new bolts of flowered silk Margaret had brought from New York. Mikal had delivered them himself yesterday afternoon, and word of the new merchandise spread quickly through the village.

An hour later, Amy was so busy waiting on customers, sketching designs, and planning summer gowns that she was only vaguely aware of Alex when he dashed in to have his breakfast. A few minutes later, he rushed back out the door, slate and lunch bucket in hand, calling over his shoulder, "Bye, Mama. See you this afternoon."

"My, how that boy has grown," one of the ladies remarked.

"Yes, hasn't he?" Amy agreed. *He's growing in more ways than one*, Amy mused silently. She wondered about the significance in the sudden improvement in her son's personal grooming and his attitude toward school. But she didn't have long to think about it, because two ladies stood in line to have pieces cut from bolts of fabric they had selected. "How many yards will I need to have a dress made like this one?" The smartly dressed woman used one hand to point to a design in the fashion book while the other kept a tight grip on a bolt of yellow dimity.

Amy pulled a stub of a pencil from behind her ear and did some quick calculations. "I'd say about nine yards, Ma'am, if you want the skirt nice and full."

"Oh, yes, and I may decide to have a matching parasol. Why don't you go ahead and give me ten, just to be on the safe side?"

While Amy measured and cut, the chatter in the room grew louder as more women crowded into the small shop. Amy usually turned a deaf ear to the endless gossip that took place in the shop each day, but the mention of Mrs. Simpson captured her attention.

"Yes, she was quite tearful about Mattilou insisting on having her hair trimmed. I'd think she'd be relieved at not having to twist all those long candlestick curls around her fingers every day."

"Why did the child want her hair trimmed?" another asked. "I thought it was quite fetching the way it hung down to her waist."

"That's what her mother thought too. But it seems Mattilou has a beau, and she decided the curls were too babyish. Now she just brushes all that thick hair down on her shoulders and lets it hang loose." The bearer of this news relished her moment of attention, smacking her lips as she revealed her cache of information.

"A beau? Who is he?" Several women asked the question at once, crowding about the news bearer to hear her answer.

"That's a mystery. Even her mother doesn't know, though she's certainly tried to find out," the lady said. "Little Mattilou won't reveal her secret to anyone."

Amy tried to turn her attention back to the customer standing at her counter. Was what she was thinking even possible? She sorely doubted it. But on the other hand, it would explain many things.

She flipped the pages of *Godey's Lady's Book* and pointed to one of the gowns. "Here's one you might like," she suggested to the fashionably dressed lady who stood next in line at the counter. "And there's a pretty burnoose to wear with it when the weather turns cooler."

Shortly before noon, the tinkling doorbell announced Margaret's arrival. "Hello, everyone." She used her handkerchief to wipe beads of perspiration from her brow before she stepped behind the counter to place her reticule on a shelf. "Did I hear someone talk about cooler weather? I hope so!"

"No time soon, I think," Amy said, perspiration trickling down her own neck. "But I expect you feel the summer heat more than usual this year."

"That's certainly true," Margaret agreed. Behind the counter, she had a chance for a few private words with Amy. "Do you think it's all right for me to come in here to work now that my condition is showing? I know many women stay at home for the last months of their confinement. I don't want to be an embarrassment to you, Amy."

"Oh, please!" Amy protested. "How could any of us be embarrassed by your wonderful gift from God? And besides, I can't handle this shop alone."

Their conversation was interrupted by the plea of a frantic customer. "Oh, Margaret. I'm so glad you're here this morning. Amy just helped me plan this extraordinary dimity gown for a garden party next month, and I simply must have one of your fancy bonnets to wear with it."

"See what I mean?" Amy whispered. "You'll be making hats with one hand and rocking the cradle with the other." Both women laughed and gave their full attention to the customers.

When noon approached, the crowd had not diminished. "We can't close for the dinner hour today," Amy said. "We can't simply push these ladies out the door. And look. There's even a man or two looking through the new books. Are you sure you're up to this, Margaret?"

"Of course," Margaret insisted.

But in spite of her friend's protests, Amy was concerned about the increasing pallor of Margaret's cheeks.

"You run along and have dinner with Mikal, and I'll handle the shop until you get back."

Margaret thought about her offer but declined. "No, Mikal won't be home for dinner today. He's loading produce onto the schooner to deliver to Mobile. A group of farmers hired him to take a short run of summer vegetables to the Alabama market. The shipment was scheduled to go to Saint Joseph, but their port is still under quarantine because of the yellow fever epidemic."

"Oh, that's so alarming. I do hope the dreaded disease doesn't reach Apalachicola."

Margaret gave her a mournful look and dropped her voice to a whisper. "I'm afraid it already has, Amy. John tells us he had to hang out two yellow flags last week. Mikal would like for me to stay in the house all the time to avoid exposure, but I just can't do that. You know I've never been one to sit in the rocking chair when there's work to be done." She pressed her forefinger to her lips as a customer approached, and Amy moved to the bookshelves. She knew better than to spread such frightening news.

At last the crowd waned. Only two customers remained, and they were both busy looking over the new supply of buttons.

"Now, Margaret, you can go," Amy urged. "Go home, have a nice dinner, and take a nap. I can hold things together until you get back."

"I have a better idea," Margaret said. "Let's put up the 'Closed' sign, and we'll both go. You need a break too; and the way I've been falling asleep in the afternoons, I may not get back before it's time to close."

"But the customers—" Amy started to protest.

"They can wait. Dresses and hats and books aren't emergencies, you know. I'm afraid we've been spoiling our customers, but we shouldn't neglect our own needs completely."

Without further protest, Amy hung up the sign while Margaret waited on the last two customers, who purchased only a few buttons.

"Walk home with me, Amy," Margaret invited. "Since Mikal won't be home for dinner, we'll have the place to ourselves. I can show you the new things I've gotten for the baby."

"Are you sure that's not too much trouble? You really should be using the time to rest."

"Nonsense. I'll be resting while we visit. I have some cold chicken left from last night's supper. Since Mikal bought me that new icebox, I can actually keep things like that for a day or two. It's so nice to be living in modern times."

Amy ran upstairs to grab her reticule. She'd stop at the general store on the way home and get a few things for supper. She didn't have an icebox, but a piece of salt pork would go nicely with a mess of fresh collard greens from the garden, especially if she cooked a few sweet potatoes to go with them.

It was a short walk to the Lees' house on Chestnut Street. As they passed by Trinity Church, Amy cast a wistful glance at the bench beneath the magnolia tree where she and Charles had sat in the moonlight just a few hours before, sharing the burdens of their hearts. She forced her eyes away from the spot and continued walking with her head held high. She had no intention of sharing her secrets, even with her best friend.

Soon they were climbing the wooden steps of the Lees' new home. Amy loved the wide veranda, complete with inviting cane-bottomed rocking chairs. Shadows danced across the cypress flooring as massive oak trees provided shade from the noonday heat. Margaret unlocked the front door and held it wide for Amy to enter.

Once they were inside, Margaret opened all the windows and let the refreshing breeze sail through the house, billowing her organdy curtains and filling the rooms with cool, salty air. She used a sharp pick to chip slivers of ice from a block in her new icebox and gave her guest a glass of the coldest water Amy had ever tasted.

"Let's sit here in the kitchen," Margaret suggested. "It's much cozier than the dining room."

Amy helped her set the table and put out the food. Along with cold slices of tender chicken, Margaret served fresh, sliced tomatoes from her garden, sweet, creamy cottage cheese, and slices of homemade, whole-wheat sourdough bread. Amy had to decline a slice of pecan pie for dessert. "It looks delicious, but I didn't save room for anything else."

"Well, at least we'll have coffee," Margaret insisted, pointing to the stove where her enamel coffeepot pulsated rhythmically, sending up a delicious aroma of the treat yet to come. Amy seldom made coffee in her upstairs quarters during the heat of the summer days; but sitting here in a crosscurrent of the brisk gulf breeze, the offer was irresistible.

Until now, almost all conversation had been about the upcoming blessed event, but over steaming cups of coffee, Margaret turned the conversation to Amy. "So, Amy, tell me what you've been up to while I've been away. Have you seen anything of that new caretaker Mikal hired?"

Amy feared her pink cheeks would give her away. "I do see Mr. Drake now and then. I believe Mikal asked him to keep an eye on the shop in his absence."

Margaret laughed. "Aren't you getting a bit formal? *Mr. Drake?* I though we all called him Charles."

"Oh, yes. Yes, of course. I meant to say Charles. He–he seems to take his work very seriously." Amy lifted her cup to her lips and hoped the subject would end there, but Margaret persisted.

"Has he completely recovered from his bout with malaria? John says it has a way of recurring. As I recall, he was quite weak when we left."

"I believe he is much stronger now. Margaret, I do want to get your recipe for pecan pie. Yours always tastes much better than mine."

Again Margaret laughed, and Amy knew she was as transparent as a piece of isinglass. "I'm glad he's stronger," Margaret said, "but what I really wanted to know was if you and he had become, um, friendly. Mikal and I discussed it while we were away. We both thought the two of you seemed to be attracted to each other."

Amy almost spilled her coffee. "Really, Margaret, I'm disturbed that you and Mikal couldn't have found a more interesting subject to talk about. Yes, Charles and I are friends, but that is all."

"Sorry, Amy. I can tell you aren't ready to talk about this. I promise not to pry into your private life anymore." Margaret sipped her coffee and dabbed at her lips with a linen napkin. "I'll copy that recipe for pecan pie and give it to you next time you're here."

Relieved to end the conversation, Amy pushed her chair back from the table. "Everything was delicious, Margaret, and I hate to eat and run, but I really should get back to open the shop."

"You can't go until you see how Mikal has fixed the baby's room," Margaret protested. "Besides, I'm really in a mess with those booties I'm knitting, and you promised to help me."

Amy chuckled. "Of course I'll help. But we still have plenty of time for that." She carried their dishes to the sink and rinsed them while Margaret put the rest of the food away. "Come on and show me the baby's room, and then I really must leave."

Margaret led the way into a small bedroom, and Amy had to struggle to suppress her amusement. Mikal had painted a border of various kinds of boats and ships all around the pale blue walls—a border that would look pretty silly if the baby turned out to be a girl. "It's. . .it's, um, unusual, isn't it?" she said, trying to come up with a tactful comment. "I can tell he's put a lot of work into this."

"Indeed he has," Margaret proudly admitted. "His latest project is a toy train. He's carving it out of a block of cherry he brought back on our last trip. I declare, I've never seen him so excited about anything as he is this baby."

"Of course he is," Amy said, picking up her reticule. "And I'm excited for both of you." She gave Margaret a light kiss on the cheek before she started for the front door. "Now, you go take that nap, and I'll take care of the shop. Afternoons aren't usually as busy as mornings, and Rachel and Priscilla will be in at two to help with the cutting for our new orders."

## sixteen

Amy woke early on the morning of the Sabbath. She sat at her small desk, poring over her worn leather Bible, a pencil tucked behind her ear. With the help of a copy of *Cruden's Concordance* from the bookshelves downstairs, she searched every reference it listed regarding forgiveness. She had asked God to make her an instrument to heal Charles's hardened heart against his enemies, but she knew God expected her to do her part too.

Alex slept on his cot nearby, his cherubic face still glowing from last night's scrubbing. How he hated those baths! She'd have to wake him soon to do a few basic chores before dressing for church.

She flipped through her Bible to the parable of the unforgiving servant that ended with the words of Christ: "So likewise shall my heavenly Father do also unto you, if ye from your hearts forgive not every one his brother their trespasses." Those words from Matthew 18:35 carried a dire warning for an unforgiving heart. She made note of the reference on a piece of paper, and her list grew longer as she continued her perusal.

She hadn't decided how or when she would present her findings to Charles; but if this was what God wanted her to do, He would surely provide a way.

Alex stirred, prompting Amy to call, "Time to get up, Son. Go downstairs and fetch a pail of clean water, and check the hen's nest while you're there. If you find an egg, I'll cook it for your breakfast."

"Yes'm." Alex rubbed his eyes and slung one leg over the side of the bed. Amy didn't prod him into action. There was still plenty of time, and she enjoyed seeing him have one morning in the week when he didn't have to hurry.

Amy put the teakettle on the stove to boil water for a cup of sassafras tea. She pulled her spider from the shelf and set it on the cast-iron stove. She'd mix up some johnnycakes while the pan heated, and when it was sizzling hot, she'd be ready to pour the batter onto it. She and Alex would have a fine breakfast of johnnycakes, sorghum, and applesauce; and if Alex was lucky enough to find an egg, she'd fry that on the spider too.

⁂

Two hours later, Amy and Alex walked side by side up the walk to the steep stone steps of Trinity Church. "Listen to those bells, Alex. Aren't they beautiful?"

"Yes'm," Alex agreed. "Sure wouldn't seem like the Sabbath without them bells."

"*Those* bells, Dear. Do try to be more careful about your grammar. Did you bring a clean handkerchief?"

"Yes'm." Alex accompanied her inside and down the aisle to a pew near the front. They shared a hymnal as the organ began to sound the chords of the opening hymn. Amy was glad Alex liked to sing. What he lacked in tone, he made up for in volume, and some of the people sitting around them smiled at his youthful exuberance. "Amazing Grace" was one of Amy's favorites too, and she raised her voice along with the congregation on every verse.

Halfway through the second verse, Margaret slid into the pew beside her and added her voice to the song. Amy smiled and reached over to give her hand a friendly squeeze. It was quite unusual to see Margaret in church without her attentive husband, but Amy remembered that Mikal hadn't returned from Mobile.

When the pastor began his sermon, Amy was stunned to learn that his topic was "Loving the Unlovable." His entire sermon centered on love and forgiveness. He even used some of the same Scripture she had noted in her early morning Bible study. She wished Charles could have heard the pastor's stirring words, especially the passage from Hebrews: "Vengeance belongeth unto me, I will recompense, saith the Lord. And again, The Lord shall judge his people." If only Charles could release his hate and vengeance and turn his heart back to God. Amy would continue to lift him up in her prayers, for as she had told Charles, with God all things are possible.

After the closing hymn, Pastor Robert pronounced the benediction and the crowd began to file out. Movement was slow because Sunday morning was a time of visitation and often the only time neighbors from opposite sides of town saw each other.

"When is Mikal due to return?" Amy asked Margaret as they inched their way toward the door.

"I'm never sure, but probably—Amy, look! Isn't that Charles Drake going out the door?"

Amy stood up on tiptoes to see over the crowd; but from her height of barely over five feet, all she could see was the backs of the people in front of her. "I don't know, Margaret. I—I hardly think so, but. . .oh, let's hurry out of here and see."

But hurrying was impossible. By the time they reached the sidewalk, whoever Margaret had seen was out of sight. Amy strained her eyes in the direction of the waterfront; and she did see a few people walking that way, but she couldn't possibly identify anyone from this distance.

"I'm quite sure it was Charles," Margaret insisted. "I recognized Mikal's blue homespun shirt, the one he gave to Charles."

"Almost every man in town owns at least one blue home-spun shirt," Amy rationalized. "Was that the only thing you recognized?"

"No, it was a tall man with sandy hair, and he walked like Charles; but of course, I only saw him from the back. Anyway, it doesn't matter, does it? Come on, let's go over here and see Frances Clark's new baby boy." She pulled Amy by the arm, and Alex ran off to join some of his friends.

*Doesn't matter? Of course it matters very much. It just might mean that Charles is beginning to turn his heart back to God, just as I've been praying for.* But Amy held her tongue and went to admire the latest addition to the Clark family.

After making all the proper comments about the new baby, Amy turned to look for her son. "Alex? Where are you?"

The question had no sooner left her lips before Alex came running up to her with Joshua, one of his best friends. Amy couldn't understand how one young boy could walk out of church looking like a picture out of her fashion magazines and turn up just minutes later with his shirttail hanging out, his hair tousled, and a grass stain smeared across his only white shirt. "Alex, what have you been doing?"

"Mama, Josh's mama invited me to eat dinner with them today. Can I, Mama? Please?"

"Looking like that? I don't think so, Alex. And besides, I thought we were going to have a picnic today down in the old walnut grove beside the creek." Seeing his crestfallen expression, Amy felt a twinge of guilt. The picnic had been her idea of a way to fill a lonely Sunday afternoon. Of course a day with his best friend would be more fun for Alex. Joshua's parents lived on a farm on the outskirts of town where the boys could ride horses and play in the open fields. She shouldn't deprive him of such a nice opportunity. "Oh, all right, Alex, if you can run home and change clothes first. I wouldn't want you to play all afternoon in your Sunday clothes."

Joshua had been hopping up and down, waiting for her answer. "That's fine, Mrs. McCutcheon. Alex has time to go home and change. My folks are still visiting with friends anyway. When they get ready to go, I'll have my dad drive the wagon by your place and pick Alex up. My mama said we can bring him back home tonight when we come in town for the evening service."

Alex had already started to make a run for home. "Wait, Alex." He halted and turned back to hear her words. "Now you be polite, you hear me? And wait to be excused from the table, and don't forget to tell Mrs. Williams you enjoyed the meal."

"Aw, Mama, I know all that stuff already. I better hurry or I'll miss my ride."

In spite of his squirming to avoid it, Amy grabbed him and planted a kiss on his cheek. "Have fun, Alex. I'll miss you."

His only reply was a mile-wide grin before he dashed off down the street toward home.

❧

Amy had no desire to go on a picnic by herself. Instead she ate a light lunch at her kitchen table and tried to plan her afternoon.

She had many things that needed doing, but activities were limited on the Sabbath, and Amy always strictly adhered to its demands. She enjoyed reading, and the bookshelves were filled with good literature; but today the weather seemed too nice to waste indoors. Perhaps she would take a walk through the woods, although she still remembered Margaret's tale about the day she'd met an Indian in those woods. He had scared Margaret silly; but in the end, he had saved her life when she fell into the creek and couldn't swim. Whenever Margaret talked about that experience, she always called it one of the turning points in her life.

It was too early in the year for walnuts. *Perhaps*, Amy thought, *I can find some wild berries to pick*. A blackberry cobbler for supper would be delicious. She changed into a faded calico dress and pulled a gingham sunbonnet from the shelf. Armed with a small tin pan for her berries, she set off toward the creek.

It was so pleasant outdoors. Birds and butterflies flew overhead, and the scent of wild roses filled the air. If she didn't find any berries, she'd take back some flowers and arrange them in a vase for the shop. She began to hum as she strolled along.

A noise from behind caught her attention, and she stopped to listen. A twig snapped and leaves rustled. Something was definitely approaching. Amy had heard tales of bears in these woods. Had she been foolish to venture so far from town? She positioned herself behind a huge oak tree and peered around its trunk, but she saw nothing. She stooped to pick up a piece of broken limb from the ground—not a very effective weapon in the face of real danger, but perhaps it could scare off a small animal.

There! She heard it again. Footsteps, and they were getting closer by the minute. Amy drew back behind the tree and raised her makeshift weapon above her head just moments before a figure emerged from the dense brush. "Charles!"

"Amy? What are you doing out here in the woods by yourself?"

Amy couldn't decide whether to be embarrassed or mad or relieved—or all three. "Did you follow me here?" she asked, dropping her stick and putting her hands on her hips.

"Of course not. How could I possibly know you'd be here? But I must say, it's a delightful surprise to find you. What are you doing out here?"

Amy's heart began to hammer at an alarming rate. Was it from the fright he had given her, or was it simply the reaction that was becoming more and more familiar in his presence? "I'm taking an afternoon walk, looking for berries if I happen to be lucky. How about you? Why are you here?"

"I'm taking a walk too. I have a lot of things on my mind, and my room at the warehouse isn't the ideal place to sort out my thoughts. I usually walk along the waterfront to meditate, but I wanted to avoid the crowds today. I learned of these woods when I came through them on my first trip to town. I find them very peaceful, don't you?"

"Yes, I do. Well, I don't want to detain you, Charles. I know you're seeking privacy. I'm walking much slower than you, so go right ahead. I'm going to search for berries." She forced her gaze from his face and continued sauntering through the woods.

In two long strides, he was beside her. "I'm very good at berry picking. Do you mind if I join you?"

"You may come if you choose," she demurred. "Look, I think I see some over there."

"Careful," he warned. "Snakes like those blackberry bushes too."

Working side by side, they had her pan filled in a short time with the biggest, juiciest blackberries Amy had ever set her eyes on. "Let's take these home and wash them. I'll find a tin and give you half."

"Oh, well I had something else in mind," Charles confessed.

"Well, of course. I know you picked more than half. You can have as many as you like," Amy told him.

Charles laughed. "That wasn't what I had in mind at all. I thought if you took them all, perhaps you would make them into something delicious; and then if I happened by your shop tomorrow evening, perhaps you would offer me a treat."

Amy felt the blood rising to her face. "Why yes, of course. I had planned to make a cobbler. Perhaps if you came by the shop about sunset, I'd be finished work for the day, and we could have coffee and dessert together." Was this the opportunity God was sending so that she might share her list of Scripture verses with Charles? She handed him the pan of berries to hold while she brushed her skirts to free them of leaves and debris before they started toward home.

"It's still light at sunset," he reminded her. "I don't want my visit tomorrow to feed the gossipmongers and cause you any embarrassment, Amy."

"Charles, I have only myself and God to answer to. My choice of guests in my home is my own business. My conscience will not trouble me, and neither should yours."

A smile spread across his sun-bronzed face, revealing perfectly spaced white teeth. "My conscience has never been a significant problem for me where you're concerned, Amy."

Looking up into his intense blue eyes, Amy felt her hammering heart skip a beat. His gaze met hers and locked for a breathtaking moment before he lowered his lips to meet her upturned face, and Amy was lost in the sweetness of his kiss.

"I–I think we should be starting back," she stammered, trying to bring her mind into focus.

"As you wish," he said, reluctantly rising and pulling her to her feet. "I hope my kiss didn't offend you. There are so many things I want to say to you, Amy dear, and so many reasons why I can't say them—at least not at this time."

"I'm not offended, Charles. And I want you to know I value your. . .your friendship more than I can tell you." She reached for the berry pan, avoiding his eyes lest she reveal too much of her feelings—feelings which definitely exceeded friendship. But she must resist the temptation to tell him so. God had outlined a plan for her, and she didn't think it included kissing! "I'm going home now, but you should continue your walk in the woods where you can meditate in privacy the way you'd planned."

Without waiting for his response, she hurried back the way she had come. Behind her, she heard his deep bass voice carried on a breath of summer wind. " 'Til tomorrow evening, then. Thank you for a lovely afternoon."

# seventeen

No more school for three whole wonderful months! Alex McCutcheon stood on the shore to toss a shell and watch it splash into the frothy blue Gulf of Mexico. He had sold all his morning newspapers by sunup, and now the whole glorious day stretched before him like a gift. His mama said each new day was a gift from God. Some days he wasn't so sure, but today really did remind him of a mysterious present waiting to be unwrapped.

He lingered on the waterfront, watching a gull swoop down to claim a fish for his breakfast. Maybe he would try his own hand at fishing today. His mama would be proud if he brought home a nice speckled trout for supper or even a whitey. Mullet was her favorite, but they were almost impossible to catch on a hook. Mullet liked to jump and splash in the water, just teasing a boy to try and catch them; but without a net, Alex knew better than to even attempt it.

The money in the jar beneath his cot grew slowly during the school year, but summer was a perfect time to speed its growth with odd jobs. Maybe he should go over to the general store and see if any of the ladies wanted their groceries carried home. Alex had a strong back, and he thought of that as an easy way to earn a few coins.

Just as he was about to walk away from the shoreline, Alex noticed a man approaching—a man he had never seen around town before. A deep purple scar down the left side of his face pulled his mouth to one side, giving him the appearance of a permanent sneer. He wore a pair of fancy boots, and he made a straight path toward Alex. "Hey there, Pardner," the man said.

Alex looked over his shoulder to see if the man could be talking to someone else, but seeing no other, he answered., "Howdy, Sir."

The man drew alongside Alex and spoke in lowered tones. "Say, you look like a smart lad. How would you like to earn a gold coin?"

"Gold?" Alex had never owned a gold coin in his entire life. "What would I have to do to earn it?" he asked skeptically.

"Well, er, you see, Son, this here is a very confidential matter. You'd be working for the, um, the U.S. government. But I gotta know you can keep secrets."

Alex felt so excited, he could hardly get the words out of his mouth. "Yes, Sir, I can sure keep secrets. I know lots of secrets, and I don't never tell nobody. What kind of secret would you want me to keep?"

The man glanced over his left shoulder and then his right to make certain their conversation was not being overheard. "Right about sundown tomorrow, I need you to be on the porch of the general store. I'm gonna come out and give you a sack, and you're to deliver the sack down to the stables at Brown Creek. You know where that is?"

"Yes, Sir." Alex knew his mama would never allow him to go to the Brown Creek stables alone, but the vision of a gold coin danced in his mind. Maybe if he could just explain to her that it was for the U.S. government, she might—

"You gotta swear not to tell no one. Not your best friend nor your mama and daddy or no one. You understand?"

Mama didn't like him to hide things from her, but since this was for the U.S. government, it must be all right. Alex felt lucky to be selected for this honor. He might even get his name in the newspaper. Wouldn't that be something? "Yes, Sir. I understand. I'll be standing on the porch of the general store at sundown tomorrow. You can count on me."

The man smiled at Alex, and Alex wondered why such an important government man had such rotten-looking teeth. Maybe his mama let him eat too much candy when he was growing up. Alex made a silent promise to himself that he would not spend his newly acquired wealth on candy. He watched the man disappear into a crowd of people at the wharf and imagined a dozen different things he could do with a real gold coin.

⋈

Even in the summer, Mondays were always busy in Margaret's Millinery Shoppe and Bookstore. Amy was glad for the extra work that kept her mind from dwelling on the evening ahead.

Upstairs her blackberry cobbler rested on the table, covered with a net to make sure no flies could spoil her culinary work of art. Alex had teased for a bowl of it at breakfast this morning, but she had held him off, promising him a generous serving after supper tonight.

In spite of her best efforts, her thoughts strayed back to the stolen kiss beside the creek yesterday. The taste of it still lingered on her lips, making her jump when a customer said, "Mrs. McCutcheon, I know what you've been doing!" Amy's head spun. Surely her blush must have given her away before the woman added, "You've been making a blackberry pie. It's almost impossible to get rid of those stains, isn't it?"

Amy gasped in relief and examined her dark fingers. She had scrubbed them over and over again with lye soap and a brush, but still a blue shadow remained. "Yes, it is," she admitted. "Almost impossible." She picked up a pair of scissors and willed her hands to quit shaking.

By late afternoon, with the help of Margaret, Rachel, and Priscilla, all the customers had been served, and at last Amy was ready to close the shop for the day. She flipped through a stack of sketches and orders and turned to the young cutters. "We'll begin working on these tomorrow, girls, so let's try to get an early start."

Priscilla and Rachel, glad for the extra work, readily agreed. Margaret, who had worked the entire day, stayed to help Amy clean up.

Through the window, Amy could see the afternoon sun sinking slowly toward the horizon. Just minutes from now it would be setting in the western sky. "Run along, Margaret. You need to take care of yourself, especially now. I can finish the rest of this." She pushed her broom across the floor, sweeping up threads and ravels along with dust and grime from the street.

Margaret retrieved her reticule from beneath the counter and pulled out an embroidered handkerchief to wipe her brow. "If you're sure, Amy. I am a bit tired. I think it's the heat more than the work. But I'll be back in the morning, ready to start on those new hat orders. I'm grateful for all these orders, but it does require a lot of work."

Amy walked her to the door and locked it behind her. She would just barely have time to wash her face and brush and braid her hair before her visitor arrived. Margaret and Mikal had running water in their new home. How nice it would be to take a bath anytime she wanted one. Instead, she had to content herself with a quick sponge bath from the pitcher and basin on her nightstand.

She did not feel comfortable inviting Charles up to her living quarters, since the one big room served as kitchen, dining room, and bedroom. Instead, she would have to fix their refreshments on a tray and serve them on one of the cutting tables. It would be an inconvenience, of course, but at least it would not strain the bands of propriety.

During the afternoon, Alex had raced into the shop and up the stairs, bubbling over with some kind of excitement.

She had tried to ask him about it, but he hurried up the stairs before she could get an answer. Perhaps now she could talk to him and find out what had happened.

She found Alex bent over a piece of paper, making some kind of notes that looked like figures. "What are you doing, Son?"

Alex looked like he had been caught with his hand in the cookie jar. He jumped up and crammed the paper into his pocket. "Nothing. Just practicing my ciphering."

Would wonders never cease? She would have expected him to be glad for a three-month respite from reading, writing, and especially arithmetic. She hadn't told him yet that she planned to have him read several books over the summer months to improve his reading skills. She'd save that surprise for later.

"We'll have supper a little later than usual tonight, Alex. I'm expecting a visitor in a short while. Have you done your chores yet?"

Alex was expected to empty the pails and bring up fresh water every day and chop enough oak to fill the wood box beside the cookstove. He seldom complained about his duties, accepting them as part of his lifestyle. "No, Ma'am. I'll get to it right now." He stood up and pushed his chair from the table. "After chores, can I have some of that cobbler, or do I have to wait 'til after supper?"

Amy smiled and tweaked his cheek. "I'll fix a bowl for you right now. I'll leave it here on the table, and you can have it as soon as your work is done."

With that incentive, Alex bounded down the stairs, carrying a pail of dirty water in each hand. Amy watched him go, marveling at his youthful energy.

❧

Charles sat across the cutting table from Amy, savoring every bite of the delicious blackberry cobbler. "Best I ever ate," he declared, placing his spoon on his plate and wiping his lips with a napkin.

Amy had purposely arranged the two chairs on opposite sides of the table to prevent any temptation to distract her. She was a woman on a mission, and she had asked God that her words would be digested with as much relish as the blackberry cobbler.

She pulled a list from her pocket and handed it to Charles, praying he would not be offended at her boldness. "I've given a lot of thought to the conversation we had the other night, Charles, and I took the liberty of making some notes on some verses I hope might help to soften the burden you carry in your heart."

Charles took the paper and studied it for several minutes by the light of the tallow candle. Amy held her breath and prayed.

"Thank you for your trouble, Amy. I see some of the same Scripture verses the pastor quoted in his sermon Sunday morning."

*So he had been in church Sunday! That surely must be a sign of changes to come.* "I do hope you'll give these verses some thought. It's not good to carry so much hate in your heart. And in the end, it really hurts only you."

"I know that," Charles admitted, "and believe me, I'm working on my attitude. I've met with Pastor Robert a few times, and he's trying to help me see things with a clear eye. For what it's worth, I'm really trying, Amy, but I can't promise anything at this point."

"I'm not asking for promises, Charles. All I want you to do is to open your heart to God's love, and He will do the rest."

Charles shook his head and stared at the paper he still held in his hands. "A love that let my mother die in my arms?" Amy heard the bitterness in his voice and saw the paper tremble in his hands.

She reached across the table to cover his hands with her

own. "Nothing in the Bible promises us that life will be easy or even fair. What it does promise is that Jesus will walk beside you through all your troubles so that you will never have to face them alone."

Charles waited for several minutes before he quietly withdrew his hands from her grasp and tucked the paper in his shirt pocket. If he agreed with her statement, Amy could detect no indication of it.

"Thank you for a wonderful dessert and especially for your thoughtful work on my behalf." He patted his shirt pocket to indicate the paper he carried. Amy followed him to the door; and when he turned to bid her good night, she turned her face up to meet his gaze. If she anticipated a good-night kiss, she was disappointed, because Charles merely shook her hand and bid her good-bye.

"Sleep well," he said and disappeared through the doorway into the twilight of evening.

# eighteen

Alex arrived on the porch of the general store an hour ahead of time. He didn't want to chance missing the government man who was depending on him to deliver a package.

Alex wondered what the package would contain. Maybe a message to the president or maybe a secret map or something to do with catching the rustlers that hid out in the territory. One thing was certain: Whatever was to be in the package was terribly important.

Alex's legs began to grow weary from standing in one spot, so he hoisted himself onto an overturned barrel and waited. One of his mother's friends came out of the store loaded down with groceries.

"Alex McCutcheon!" she declared. "This must be my lucky day. Can you take some of these groceries to my house for me?" She winked at him and added coyly, "I think I just happen to have a few shiny pennies in my purse."

Alex slid down from the barrel and squirmed. "Um, I sure would like to help you, Miz Collins, but I done promised to—" Alex caught himself before he revealed too much. "I–I can't today. I'm awful sorry, Ma'am."

The woman gave him a curious stare. "Very well then, Alex. I'm sorry to have troubled you."

Alex watched her struggle down the steps with her groceries. He could tell she was peeved with him, but what choice did he have? Anyway, after all this was over, she would likely hear about the important job he had done for the government, and then she would understand why he hadn't been able to help her.

He climbed back onto the barrel and waited. The sun had already set, and it was growing dark. Mama would set out to look for him if he didn't get home before long. Could the man have been trying to play a trick on Alex? He sounded serious enough at the time.

Just when Alex was about to give up and go home, he heard a sound from around the corner of the store. *Psst!* He looked but saw no one. He waited for a few seconds, and then he heard it again. *Psst!* This time he walked to the edge of the porch and peered around the corner.

To his great surprise, the government man crouched down in the bushes that grew beside the porch. "Here, Sonny. I'll leave the bag here in the bushes for you to get after I'm gone. Just give me a few minutes, and then it's time for you to do your job."

Things were not going exactly the way Alex had expected. "What about my gold coin?" he asked.

The man reached into the bag and pulled out a beautiful, shiny gold dollar. He held it up for Alex to see. "Here, Son. This is yours to keep." He thrust the coin into Alex's hand. "Now, get on with your work before somebody gets hurt." The man disappeared through the shrubbery so quickly that Alex wondered for a moment if he had imagined the whole scene. But then he felt the cold, hard coin in his hand and knew he was not dreaming. Alex thrust the treasure into his pants pocket and jumped down into the bushes to pick up the bag.

The canvas bag was heavier than it looked and dirty too. It seemed to Alex that the government should at least provide clean bags for people who carried their secrets. Alex looked both ways before he slung the bag over his shoulder. Seeing people gathered in clusters on the porch and a group of men on horseback bunched together at the far end of the street, Alex decided to use the deserted alley behind the store. He took off toward the north, in the direction of the stables at Brown Creek.

He ran at first, but the weight of the bag soon forced him to slow down. He couldn't stop, though. The government man was depending on him. He plodded down the dusty street.

Two blocks beyond the general store, he heard a loud, angry voice. "Stop, thief!" Alex looked around, expecting to see a thief making a getaway; but all he saw was Mr. Diamanti, still wearing his bloodstained butcher apron and three other men Alex recognized as Apalachicola businessmen. They were waving their hands in the air and screaming, and still Alex didn't see who they were chasing.

He stopped under a spreading oak tree to let them pass, but instead, they bore down on him with a fury the likes of which he had never seen.

A brawny man lifted Alex off his feet and into the air, his legs flailing in space; and when he did, the coveted gold coin dropped from his pocket to the ground. Mr. Diamanti picked up the gold piece and grabbed the canvas bag from Alex's hands. The storekeeper looked at him in surprise. "Alex? You? I never would have believed this if I hadn't seen it with my own eyes."

"Wait, Mr. Diamanti," Alex protested. "You can't have that bag. It's. . .I can't tell you what it is. It's a secret, but I've gotta deliver it." He kicked at the man who held him aloft. "Put me down. I'm working for the United States government." He hadn't meant to tell, but everything was going all wrong.

"Yeah, and I'm the king of England," the brawny man said. Several of the men laughed at this, but Mr. Diamanti looked terribly sad. A crowd began to gather around the scene of such excitement, and one of the men said, "Somebody get the sheriff. He's got a place for thieves like this."

"You don't understand," Alex kept protesting. Tears streamed down his face. Didn't anybody hear him say he was working for the government? "I'm not a thief," he insisted over and over again, even as he was being dragged through the streets toward the jail on the edge of town.

❧

Amy had closed the shop and sent everyone home, but where was Alex? Now that school was over, he was becoming harder to keep track of. He knew her rule about being home by dark. Where was he at this hour? She went to the steps and peered up and down the street in both directions.

A rider approached on horseback and stopped in front of her shop. "Mrs. McCutcheon? I'm afraid I have a bit of bad news for you."

Amy felt the blood drain from her face, and she clutched the post to keep from falling to the ground. "Alex? Is Alex hurt?" She willed herself not to faint, because Alex needed her. "Where is he?"

The man held his hat in his hands and shuffled his feet in the dust. "No, Ma'am. He ain't hurt." Amy's relief was short-lived, because the man's next words were like a knife thrust into her heart. "He's in the sheriff's cooler."

"Cooler? You mean the jail?" Amy was incredulous. "You mean Alex, my little boy? That's impossible. Why would you say such a thing?"

"I'm awful sorry, Ma'am. I can see this is upsetting you, but somebody said you ought to know, so I volunteered to be the one to come tell you."

"Well, how did he get there? Who would put an innocent child in jail?" Amy's voice had risen to hysteria.

"Well, um, you oughta hear this from somebody else besides me, Ma'am, but I think he stole a bag of gold from Mr. Diamanti at the general store."

"Alex never stole anything in his life," Amy insisted. "Where is this jail you keep talking about? I demand that you take me there at once so I can get the whole matter straightened out."

"I've only got the one horse, Ma'am. I don't own a wagon. If I did, I'd be glad to take you. It's pretty far for you to walk. Is there someone I can get to come for you?"

Amy began to realize she was coming down very hard on a stranger who only volunteered to help. "Forgive me," she said. "Yes, let me think." If only Mikal were here. He'd know what to do. His schooner was due in tonight; but if he hadn't gotten home yet, she didn't want to upset Margaret with this kind of news. She thought of John Gorrie, who was always willing to help anyone in need; but he was seldom at home, especially now with all the serious illnesses sweeping through the territory. None of her friends lived nearby, and she didn't want to waste time trying to locate them. Of course Charles would help if he could, but he didn't have a wagon either. Nevertheless, she longed to have him beside her, a pillar of strength to lean on.

"Yes," she finally decided. "Please go down to Mikal Lee's warehouse on the waterfront, and see if you can find a Mr. Charles Drake. He lives in a room at the back. Just tell him what you've told me. I'm sure he'd want to know. Tell him to go to Alex, and I'll come as soon as I can. And now, if you'll point me in the direction of the jail, I'm going to start walking. Perhaps I'll see someone I know who can give me a ride."

Reluctantly, the rider told her how to get to the jail, and he promised to deliver her message to Charles Drake. He slung himself onto his horse's bare back, and in a cloud of dust, he galloped toward the waterfront.

Amy stepped out into the street and started walking. She'd beg a ride from the first wagon that passed; and if she couldn't find someone to help her, she'd walk all the way if necessary. Alex, her baby, was in trouble; he needed her.

❧

Charles sat on the edge of his cot, studying his Bible, when a knock sounded on the door. Anticipating some kind of trouble, he bounced up to open it. He had just completed his evening inspection of Mikal's properties, and he hadn't seen anything suspicious; but things could get out of hand in a hurry in this part of town, especially after the sun set.

He flung open the door and looked into the face of an obviously distraught man. The messenger related the whole story as he knew it, ending with the plea of the boy's mother. "She said to ask you to find her son and go to him, and she would come as soon as she could."

"How was she going to get there?" Charles asked. "Did she have transportation?"

"No, Sir. She started out walking, but—"

*"Walking?"* Charles gripped the man's shoulders. "It's too far for a lady to walk and much too dangerous." He reached in his pocket and pulled out some coins. "Here, take this and go down to the pier. Hire a phaeton or whatever you can find, and go look for her. Tell her I've gone to the jail to see about Alex."

He didn't wait to hear the astonished man's reply before he took off in the direction of the jail.

A few men were gathered at the entrance of the small brick building. Charles elbowed his way to the front. "I'm here to see Alex McCutcheon. Where is he?"

A ripple of laughter surrounded him. "That's what we're all here for, Mister. We all want to see what the sheriff is going to do with that kid who stole the gold from the general store."

"Where is the sheriff now?" Charles demanded.

"He's inside with the boy, but he won't let nobody else in right now. I reckon he's questioning the boy. Are you his father?"

"No, but I represent the boy and his mother." Charles rapped sharply on the jailhouse door.

A man guarding the door from the inside opened it just a

crack. "Go on home, now. We ain't gonna let nobody in here tonight."

Charles repeated his demand. "I'm here to represent Alex and his mother, Mrs. McCutcheon. I have a right to see him to find out what's going on."

"Hold on," the guard said. Presumably he left to receive his instructions from the sheriff. When he returned to the door, he opened it and said, "Come on in, but the rest of you guys, go on now. We don't want no more trouble tonight."

The jail consisted of three small cells. Alex sat on a cot in the middle one, his pale face streaked with dried tears. In front of him, a stout, bearded man sat on a stool. Charles heard him say, "All you have to do is tell us the truth, Son."

"But I am telling the truth," Alex protested. And then he looked up and saw Charles. The familiar face brought on a new spate of tears. "Mr. Drake, tell this man I'm not a thief. They say I stole Mr. Diamanti's gold, but you know I wouldn't steal nothing. Tell him, Mr. Drake."

"Hold on, Alex." The cell door was ajar, and Charles entered and sat on the cot beside Alex. He put his arm around the frightened boy and let him sob into his shirt-front. Holding Alex close, he addressed the sheriff. "Suppose you tell me what happened here."

"It's simple," the sheriff began. "Mr. Diamanti noticed his safe was ajar, and of course he checked it. When he did, he saw that the bag holding all his gold was missing. That's when he and some of his customers gave chase to this boy, who was running down the alley with the money bag. He even had one of the coins in his pocket. That's all there is to it. The boy stole money, and he got caught. Beats me how he got that safe open, though. And he sure ought to win some kind of prize for coming up with the craziest alibi I've ever heard."

Charles pulled his bandana from his pocket and used it to

wipe Alex's face. "Now, Alex, let's hear what you have to say."

"Like I told the sheriff, I was doing some secret work for the government."

"See what I mean?" The sheriff chuckled.

"Let's hear the boy out," Charles insisted. "Go ahead, Alex. How did you happen to be working for the government?" Charles did not even smile when he asked the question, which apparently encouraged Alex to continue.

"I wasn't supposed to tell anybody, but this man told me if I'd deliver this sack to the stables at Brown's Creek, he'd give me a gold coin. I didn't know what the sack had in it. I wasn't supposed to ask."

Charles turned to the sheriff. "Have you checked to see if anybody strange showed up at the stables at Brown's Creek tonight?"

"Yeah, I had a man ride down there, but he said there was nothing unusual going on. You don't really believe that wild story, do you?"

Charles ignored the sheriff and turned again to Alex. "Alex, what did this man look like? Would you know him if you saw him again?"

"Sure I would," Alex said. "He was kind of heavy, and he wore real fancy boots."

Charles digested this description. Not much to go on. "Anything else you can remember, Alex? Try hard."

"No." Alex raised his forefinger to his temple, trying to remember. "Oh, yeah, he did have kind of a funny mouth. Crooked like, you know. I think it might have come from that jagged purple scar on his face."

"Scar?" Charles jumped to attention. "Did you say he had a jagged purple scar on his face? Which side? Think hard, Alex, because this is important."

"Um, I think it was this side." Alex pointed to his left cheek. "Yep, I'm sure it was this side."

Charles tried to swallow his excitement. "Sir," he said to the sheriff, "I think you can see this boy poses no threat to anyone. If you'll let me take him home, I'll be personally responsible for him."

The sheriff laughed. "I can't do that. I know you work for Mikal Lee because I've seen you around town; but for all I know, you might be part of this crazy scheme. No, I can't give him over to you. Sorry, but the boy stays here."

"How about if I get John Go-rrie to accept the responsibility? Could you let him go then?"

The sheriff rubbed his bearded chin. "Now that's a different situation. Yes, if Dr. Gorrie wants to vouch for the boy, I reckon I could let him go until we figure out what to do with him; but he better not try to pull any tricks while he's out."

Charles held Alex against his chest. "Alex, you've got to be very brave and stay here until I get Dr. Gorrie to help us, but we'll have you out of here as quick as we can. Do you understand?"

"Yes, Sir." Alex's chin quivered, but he tried hard to put up a valiant front. "Will you tell my mama where I am? And be sure to tell her I didn't steal anything."

"She knows that, Son." He patted Alex on the shoulder before he stood up to leave. To the sheriff, he said, "Can you give me a paper to have Dr. Gorrie sign, or does he have to come down here in person?"

"I reckon I can fix up a paper for you. I know the doc is busy with all the sickness in town. But you better not bring back any counterfeit signature, or you'll both be in more trouble than you are already."

Charles was reluctant to leave Alex, but he had no choice if he wanted to get the boy released. He passed the guard at the door. "I'll return as soon as I can," he promised Alex.

Stepping out into the night air, he saw that the crowd had dispersed. Only one small, four-wheeled carriage drew up to the door; and when it stopped, Amy stepped out and fell into his arms.

"Oh, Charles. What have they done to my baby? Where is he?"

"I've talked to him, Amy, and he's going to be all right. Come with me now. We have work to do."

"Not until I see Alex. I've come all this way, and I'm not leaving until I see him."

"Amy, please trust me. Alex is safe where he is, and you need to come with me to help arrange for his release." He spoke to the driver and reached into his pocket for his dwindling supply of coins. He helped Amy climb back into the carriage, then swung up beside her.

"Where are we going?" she asked.

"To Dr. Gorrie's residence," he said to the driver, and Amy heard the answer to her own question. Charles put an arm around her shoulder, and the horses clopped away, pulling the carriage down the dusty street.

# nineteen

Charles, Amy, and Alex sat around the kitchen table in the one-room apartment over the millinery shop. Amy had ceased to worry about the propriety of having a gentleman caller in her living quarters. Her only concern at this point was how to get her son out of trouble and clear his name.

"You believe me, don't you, Mama?"

"Of course I believe you, Darling. And so does Mr. Drake. We just have to figure a way to prove it, that's all." She poured a glass of milk and put it in front of him, even though he had refused all offers of food or drink.

Charles had been unusually quiet since they got home. Amy was certain he believed Alex's story, but she wanted to know what thoughts seemed to so completely absorb him. "Have you told me everything, or is there more that I should know, Charles?"

Instead of answering her question, he asked one of his own. "Alex, tell me again what this man looked like. How tall was he? What color was his hair? And tell me more about that scar on his face."

Alex had repeated his story over and over again, and it was always the same. Alex's eyes were bloodshot, and his face was pale. It was plain to see he needed sleep, but he tried once again to describe the man who called himself a government agent; the man who had promised to give Alex a gold coin but instead had given him the biggest problem of his young life.

Amy could stand it no longer. "Alex, go to bed." She placed her hand on his forehead and decided he was not feverish.

"Try not to worry, Dear. We'll put our trust in the Lord, and everything will work out for the best. You'll see."

The child did not need a second invitation. He took off his brogans before he fell onto his cot, clothes and all, and within minutes his soft snores echoed through the room.

Oh, the blissful innocence of childhood! Amy was sure she would not sleep at all this night. She had told Charles several times how grateful she felt for his assistance, but she felt compelled to tell him again. "I don't know how I could have managed without your help, Charles. You knew just what to do. And John was kind to sign the paper accepting responsibility for Alex's behavior."

"John knows Alex is a good boy," Charles said, "and he will be very influential in seeing that Alex is treated fairly. The whole town respects John Gorrie's opinions."

"You must go now too, Charles. I know you're still not as strong as you used to be, and I fear all this might bring on a relapse of your malaria. Can I give you something to eat or drink before you go?"

"I'm fine, Amy. But what about you? Did you have supper tonight before all this came up?"

Amy looked at the pot of beans on the cold stove. She had no stomach for food this night. "No," she confessed. "I was waiting for Alex to come home when the messenger arrived. I'm afraid supper was forgotten, but I couldn't eat a bite now."

"You need to keep up your strength for Alex's sake. We aren't done with this thing yet. But I won't badger you about it. Just promise me you'll try to take care of yourself." He stood up and edged his way toward the stairs. "I have to go now, Amy, but I'll be back tomorrow. You just hang up your 'Closed' sign when you get up, and don't let anyone in."

"But what will people think when they see the shop closed?"

"Amy, Apalachicola is a very small town. Do you really think the events of tonight can be kept secret?"

"No, I suppose you're right. I'll do as you suggest." Amy followed him down the staircase, stopping at the front door to let him out. "Please go home and get some sleep, Charles. You look very tired."

He tilted her chin and brushed his lips against hers. "There'll be time to sleep later, but right now I have some unfinished business to take care of."

Amy watched him descend the front steps and disappear into the night. What was his unfinished business? She had been afraid to ask.

☙

Charles walked briskly to the Lees' residence on Chestnut Street and rattled the front door. He hoped Mikal had gotten home tonight as he had planned.

The house was bathed in darkness. The Lees would surely be asleep by now, but this wasn't a social call, and Mikal would want to know what had happened.

After a long wait, Charles finally heard footsteps and then the latch turning on the door. "Who's there?" Mikal demanded before opening it.

"It's me. Charles. Something bad happened tonight. Something you need to know about."

Mikal flung the door open wide and waved Charles inside. Behind him, Margaret appeared from the hallway, carrying an oil lamp. "Who is it, Mikal? Is something wrong?"

The three of them sat in the parlor while Charles relayed everything he knew about the events of the night. He ended by saying, "What I need from you, Mikal, is a horse. I'm going after that man. I have a strong suspicion there may be more than one of them, and I'll find them if it's the last thing I do."

"Of course I'll give you a horse, but I'm coming with you. Even if you're lucky enough to find them, you can't approach men like that by yourself. It would be suicidal."

Margaret twisted her hands together. "Oh, poor Amy. I must go to her at once."

"Begging your pardon, Ma'am, but I don't think that would be in her best interest or yours right now." Charles could see relief spreading over Mikal's face at this bit of advice. "You see, when I left there, Alex was asleep and Amy was exhausted. After a lot of protesting, she finally agreed to go to bed. I'd suggest you wait and see her in the morning. She'll need your friendship and encouragement when she wakes up; but right now, she needs her sleep even more."

"All right, if you think that's best. But I'll go over at first light and see what I can do to help."

"I need to leave now," Charles said. "You don't have to come with me, Mikal. Just show me which horse you want me to use, and I'll be on my way."

But his words might as well have not been spoken. "Time's a-wasting," Mikal said. He ran to the bedroom, reappeared in a few moments wearing dungarees and a shirt, kissed his wife, and started toward the back door.

At the door, Charles grabbed his arm and spoke in an undertone. "What about guns, Mikal? Do you have any?"

Mikal's face bore a grim expression. "I keep them locked up in a cabinet to use only for protection. I think you know my feelings about violence and killing, but in this case, you're absolutely right. We can't go after those scoundrels unarmed."

He walked back through the kitchen while Charles stood by the door waiting for him. In moments he reappeared wearing a pistol in a holster and handed Charles the same. "Strap this on and let's get going."

"Oh, Mikal, please be careful." Margaret's anguished cries followed them all the way to the stable.

"Which way do you think they would head?" Mikal asked while he and Charles saddled two horses.

"I reckon they'd have started out in the direction of Brown's Creek, but the sheriff says he sent somebody over there to check things out. They're probably already alerted, so they may have moved on. I figure they won't go too far, though, until they find out what happened to that sack of gold. I told Amy to keep Alex inside just in case they try to come back and find him."

The two men guided their mounts north following the direction of the Apalachicola River. They rode through the dense woods; for although the trees and brush made travel slower, they would help to conceal their presence.

It was necessary to ride single file through the thick undergrowth, making talk difficult. When space allowed, Mikal drew up alongside his friend and said, "Charles, I know you want to clear Alex's name; but since the gold has been returned to its rightful owner, do you really think this hunt is necessary?"

"It is for me," Charles responded. "If these men are who I think they are, there's more at stake than a bag of gold." He wouldn't burden Mikal with the details of his personal vendetta unless his suspicions proved true.

Without further discussion, they rode through the forest until they approached a clearing, where they discovered remnants of several deserted campfires. "These ashes are cold," Charles observed. "They aren't from recent fires."

"Reckon they'd make camp around here somewhere, or would they pick a spot closer to the river?" Mikal asked. "I don't know how far they planned to go before stopping, but they'd have to give their horses water and a rest sometime."

"It's a pretty sure guess they'd head for the red hills. They probably have a few hideouts there. They might even be headed for Alabama, but I still think they'd stay close enough to check on the gold once the coast is clear. They have to wonder if Alex still has it."

The moon sent shards of golden light through the overhead

canopy of leaves. Charles tried to ignore his fatigue. Malaria had reduced his stamina, and he knew he wouldn't be able to go much farther without finding a place to rest. He hadn't slept in more than twenty-four hours, but the intensity of his avenging spirit overrode his exhaustion. He couldn't give in to his body's cries for rest now.

Then an idea popped into his mind. *Why didn't I remember this in the first place?* "Mikal, there's a tavern over on the river. It's a pretty wild place—not the kind of establishment you or I would frequent—but it might be interesting to check it out to see who's there tonight."

"Won't hurt to look," Mikal agreed. "If you know where it is, lead the way."

Charles turned his horse east, and Mikal followed. When they reached the banks of the Apalachicola River, they turned north and followed the river's course until Charles stopped and pointed. "There it is yonder. See that log cabin ahead?"

Despite their agitation, they moved at a slower pace, inching their way in the shadows of giant cypress trees. Charles put his finger to his lips to signal silence, but he needn't have bothered.

Riotous laughter streamed through the open windows, along with the acrid smell of tobacco smoke and whiskey. Six horses were tied to the hitching post out front.

"That's them!" Charles could barely conceal his excitement. "We've got 'em!"

"Hold on, Fellow," Mikal said. "Not so fast. We can't handle six men—maybe more—by ourselves. It would be suicidal."

Charles drew in a deep breath and tried to slow his racing pulse. "Mikal, a month ago I'd have thought my own life would be a small price to pay for the pleasure of putting an end to those guys. But now, well, you're right. I've begun to see things in a different light. I agree we need to get some help."

Mikal heaved a sigh of relief. "We have to be sensible, Charles. We don't know if these are the men we're looking for."

"No, you don't understand, Mikal. I'm *absolutely positive* they're the men we're looking for. But I'll go along with you about the idea of getting help. I know those guys. They'll be heavily armed and ruthless. We'd better ride back to town fast and see if we can round up some lawmen to come out here and arrest them."

Mikal was still not convinced. "Charles, how can you be so sure these are the men who tried to steal Mr. Diamanti's gold? You haven't even seen them yet. And if you did see them, how would you know then? All you have to go on is a young boy's description."

"No, Mikal. I know for certain they're the outlaws we're looking for. I know because. . .because those are *my horses* tied to that hitching post!

# twenty

"It wasn't easy to convince the sheriff in Apalachicola to round up a posse to capture those outlaws," Mikal reported to the group of people seated around the table in his dining room. "But when they realized it was the notorious Washburn gang, it seemed like every man for miles around wanted a piece of the action."

In the almost twenty-four hours since the outlaws had been apprehended, the story had been told over and over again, down to the smallest details.

Declaring it a kind of celebration, Margaret had prepared a fine evening feast for Charles, Mikal, Amy, and Alex. She had invited the Gorries too, but John chose to avoid close contact with his friends to reduce the risk of carrying germs from his yellow fever patients. His wife, Caroline, was still in South Carolina.

"Our Charles is a hero," Margaret declared. "The sheriff said a U.S. marshal is coming to Apalachicola to take those men into federal custody, and they want Charles to be ready to testify against them."

"I might have to testify too," Alex stated proudly. "I know what that man looked like."

Charles remained silent while he devoured a plate of fried shrimp, but Mikal continued to heap praise on him. "Yes, the sheriff told us that men all over the Florida Territory and even into Alabama and Mississippi have been trying to break up that gang for a long time, but they haven't been able to catch up with them. I heard the sheriff say there was a substantial reward for information leading to their capture, Charles.

That'll be nice for you, but I hope this won't mean you'll be leaving my employ."

Amy's heart skipped a beat. If Charles were to receive a large amount of cash, then that is exactly what it would mean. Not only would he leave Mikal's employ, but he'd likely leave the Apalachicola area altogether and return to the red hills—and to Melinda. Amy knew she should be happy for him, but her heart ached at the thought of losing him. She had known from the beginning that his eventual departure was inevitable, but only now that the time was at hand did she feel the full impact of that truth. She looked at him across the table, memorizing his dear face to hold in her heart forever.

Then another thought occurred to her. "Doesn't the capture of these outlaws put Charles in great danger? I mean, suppose they have friends—other members of their gang—who might be out to get revenge."

Still Charles did not look up from his plate. As he ate, he seemed to be engrossed in his own thoughts, oblivious to the conversation surrounding him.

But Mikal was unusually loquacious. He seemed to enjoy reliving the exciting adventure that led to the arrest of six of the most feared outlaws in the entire Florida Territory and beyond. "When you think about it, Amy, those men should be grateful to Charles. In a way, he saved their lives."

"I don't understand how you can say that," Margaret argued. "We all know it was Charles who identified them as the men who rustled his livestock and burned his home to the ground. You told us that murder is included in their list of offenses. I believe they'd stop at nothing to get even with him."

"Indeed they do have at least one murder charge facing them," Mikal affirmed, "but they can all thank Charles that they aren't hanging from an oak tree right now. Once that angry mob got ahold of those men, the sheriff lost all control. He kept insisting he would have to lock up the outlaws in the city jail to hold until the marshal arrived; but a lot of those men who made up that posse had been victims of rustlers themselves, and they argued for their own kind of frontier justice."

"You mean—" Amy's eyes widened in horror, and she could not complete her sentence.

"I mean they wanted to have a hanging right then and there. They yelled and carried on so, the sheriff's words were lost in the uproar. Then Charles spoke up, and everyone stopped to listen because he was their hero."

"What did Mr. Drake say?" Alex asked. He had become so engrossed in Mikal's story that he was forgetting to eat his dinner.

"Well," Mikal began, and forks paused, suspended in midair, as he related details of that unforgettable night. Only Charles continued to eat, his attention obviously focused elsewhere, while Mikal told of his heroic actions. "Charles stood up on a stump and gave a rather eloquent speech. He told the sad story of how his home had been burned to the ground, his livestock stolen, and worst of all, he told them of the tragic death of his mother. The men got real quiet and circled around him to listen. He told them how at first he felt just as they did. He only wanted to find those men and inflict on them some of the pain he had endured. He confessed he would gladly have helped to hang them."

Mikal paused to take a sip of water. Not a word was spoken as everyone waited for him to continue.

"Then Charles told them how in recent weeks his life had changed. He said he had turned back to God and had asked Him to rid his heart of hate and vengeance. As he spoke, that once-riotous crowd listened in absolute silence. He told them he wanted to see justice done, and he hoped these outlaws would be put where they could never again inflict their evil deeds on innocent people. But he told them they should not take the law into their own hands. He told them it was the job of the U.S. marshal to come and take these men into custody, to hold a fair trial, and to assure that justice is delivered."

"Then what happened?" Alex prodded.

"The men in the posse helped the sheriff tie the outlaws' hands behind their backs, put them on horses, and lead them back to town."

"I thought those horses belonged to Charles," Margaret said.

"I feel certain they do," Mikal agreed, "and there's a good chance some of his herd might be recovered and returned to him too. But all that will take time to sort out. Meanwhile, it's business as usual for us, right, Charles?"

At last Charles looked up from his plate. "Right. Business as usual. And that reminds me, it's almost time for me to make my nightly inspection of your property, so if you'll all excuse me. . ." He looked to his hostess.

"Of course, Charles, but at least stay until you've had dessert. I've made a fresh guava cobbler, and remember, you are the honoree here tonight."

"Yes, Charles. Stick around awhile longer. I'll go with you to check on things later," Mikal urged.

But Charles thanked Margaret for a wonderful meal and bid them all good night. It was quite apparent he had a lot on his mind and that he preferred to be alone with his thoughts.

Mikal walked with him to the front door and lingered to speak to him, while the women exchanged glances. Of the three remaining at the table, only Alex continued to eat and chatter, his appetite seemingly stimulated by all the excitement of the evening. He helped himself to another of Margaret's buttermilk biscuits and slathered it with butter.

"Did you know about that already?" Amy asked when she was finally able to settle her mind enough to speak.

"You mean about what Charles told those men? No, Mikal hadn't mentioned that part to me. What does it mean?"

Amy had prayed for weeks that Charles would rid his

heart of hate and vengeance. Could those verses she had given him have been at least partially responsible for the change in his heart? Her own heart sang with joy at Mikal's astonishing revelations. From across the table, Margaret was looking at her, waiting for an answer to her question.

"What does it mean? I think," Amy began, then paused to decide how best to express her thoughts. "I think it means we have just witnessed a miracle!"

❧

Charles thrust his hands in his pockets and walked toward the waterfront. He always varied his route around the properties to prevent trespassers from predicting his presence. He circled the warehouse on silent feet. Seeing nothing suspicious, he turned toward the wharf where Mikal's boats were tied.

He owed so much to that man. Mikal's willingness to trust a complete stranger had given Charles a chance to forge a new life for himself here in Apalachicola. In spite of the revelation of the reward money, Charles would not walk off and leave Mikal until he found a suitable replacement for his job.

He had been awestruck when the sheriff had mentioned the amount of the bounty for the captured fugitives—more money than he would have earned in several years working in Apalachicola. And there was a good chance most of his livestock would be returned to him after the trial. Of course he hadn't done it for money. Initially he had done it solely for revenge.

But something had happened these last few weeks to change his heart. Even Charles himself had been surprised at his lack of hate when he came face-to-face with the men who had tried to destroy his life. Of course he wanted them stopped from continuing their evil actions, but he didn't hate them anymore.

Finding his way back to God was the greatest reward of all for Charles—greater than all the money in the world. These last few weeks he had been able to feel a peace and joy that had been missing from his life ever since the night of the fire. And now he had to chart a new course for his life.

As soon as he could be relieved of his duties and feel assured that Mikal's property was in good hands, he would go home to Melinda. Home? He had no home, he reminded himself; but he had a promise to keep, and keep it he would. Melinda waited for him in the red hills. He would not let her down.

But what about Amy? Before he had learned of the reward, he had felt he had nothing to offer her and no right to tell her of his love. Even now, what right did he have? What did he really have to offer her?

He couldn't stay in Apalachicola. He had an obligation to fulfill. And all he had left in the red hills was a piece of charred land. He would have to rebuild everything from the ground up. That would take many months of hard labor and use up most of the money he would receive for his part in the apprehension of the notorious Washburn gang.

He was not afraid of hard labor, and he wouldn't begrudge the expenditures. His reward would be in making Melinda smile again. He would have to put his trust in God and move forward into a new life.

He couldn't imagine a life without Amy, now that he had grown to love her so much, but she deserved so much more than he could ever offer.

She and Alex were settled into a secure and seemingly happy lifestyle in Apalachicola. Amy was a successful business-woman, and Alex was growing up into a fine young man. Nothing he could offer would compare with that.

Before he left town, he wanted to tell her just once that he loved her—would always love her—but that would only place an extra burden on her heart. It always pained Amy to hurt or disappoint anyone. Better that he bury his secret deep within his heart and ride out of her life forever.

## twenty-one

Amy was bent over the perplexing chain-stitch sewing machine with her back to the door until she heard the bell ring and turned around to see Charles standing in the threshold. Since he had become something of a hero in town, Charles had gained the respect of the Apalachicola gentry; and his friendship with Amy was now known and accepted. Some called it courtship, but Amy insisted to all who bothered to listen that her relationship with Charles was merely that of a very dear friend.

Hearing the bell ring, Amy turned around to see who had entered the shop. The sight of Charles standing in the center of the room, attired in his new clothes and boots, took her breath away. As he took long strides to cover the distance between them, women in the store pulled back and made a path for him. Scissors that had been clicking busily at the cutting tables fell suddenly silent. Amy was all too aware of the eyes focused on her burning cheeks. "Good afternoon, Charles."

He did not waste words on small talk. He cut right to the point. "Amy, I need to talk to you. Alone."

Scissors began to click again, faster than before, and women decorously turned to the shelves lined with bolts of fabric and trims.

Amy rose from her chair and raised questioning eyes to meet his. "Now, Charles? Is this something that can't wait until closing time?"

"I'm afraid it can't. Can you step outside with me for a few moments?"

Amy hesitated. The shop was filled with customers, and Margaret had gone home for the day. "Rachel," she called to the young girl at the table slicing her scissors into a piece of green bombazine. "Can you leave that for a few minutes and handle the customers while I'm out? I won't be long," she promised. "If things get to be more than you can handle alone, you can ask Priscilla to help you."

"Of course, Mrs. McCutcheon," the girl replied. She hung her scissors on a ribbon around her neck and moved to the counter. "Will you be wanting me to lock up if you're not back by quitting time?"

"I'll be back," she called over her shoulder as Charles gripped her arm and spirited her out the door.

She did not protest when he offered his arm and led her into the street. Through the sleeve of his shirt, she could feel the tense muscles of his forearm. Why did her heart react so strongly to his every touch, every nuance, no matter how subtle or casual?

"What is it, Charles? Why the urgency?" she asked as they strolled in the direction of Trinity Church.

"I'm leaving tonight, Amy, but I couldn't leave without telling you good-bye."

Amy felt suddenly dizzy and light-headed. The street beneath her feet began to spin like the winds of a tornado. Reeling, she clutched his sleeve with her free hand to keep from falling. "Tonight? Why. . .why this sudden decision?"

Then anger began to rise within her. Why had he waited until now to tell her. . .and like this? But the undeniable outpouring of love in her heart soon pushed out any traces of anger, and tears began to slide down her face.

"Amy, Dear, please don't cry. I can't bear to leave if you cry. But I must leave. We've both known all along that this was coming."

She freed her hands and swiped at her cheeks. She hadn't

meant to let him see her cry and discover how much it mattered. "Of course I knew. I just didn't think it would happen so suddenly."

As the church came into view, Charles led her to the bench where they had sat once before, sharing the secrets of their hearts. People passing by in carriages and on foot cast idle glances in their direction.

"You might have told me in a more gentle manner and in a more private place," Amy said. She still wore her work apron, and she pulled a handkerchief from her pocket to dab at her eyes.

"I'm sorry about that, but I received word only an hour ago that the U.S. marshal arrived in Apalachicola today. He wants to bring the Washburn gang to trial and get everything settled as soon as possible so he can return to the States. But first he wants me to accompany him to the Washburn camp in the red hills to identify what's left of my stolen livestock."

"So soon? Can't he give you a few days to make plans?"

"He covers a lot of territory, so he wants to get this business settled as soon as possible. They can't bring the animals back here because we don't have any holding pens for them; so once they identify them as mine, it will be up to me to find a place to keep them."

A faint hope flickered in Amy's breast. "But you'll have to come back here for the trial, won't you?"

She could anticipate his answer by the pain etched on his face. "No, I'll have to hire a crew of men in the red hills to help me construct some makeshift pens for the livestock, and then I'll have to go with the marshal to Tallahassee for the trial." His voice broke as he spoke. "So, Amy, I'm afraid this is good-bye." He tried to comfort her by gripping her hands and pulling her closer, but she pulled away from him and rose to her feet.

"What about Mikal? You said you wouldn't leave until he found someone to take your place." She was grasping at straws, but she couldn't let him leave without putting her best effort into keeping him here. "You owe quite a lot to Mikal, Charles."

"Mikal and I have talked about this, Amy. He doesn't plan to hire anyone until the next cotton crops start coming in. He wants to stay here in Apalachicola until the baby comes, so he won't be taking the *Windsong* to New York again until fall. He offered me a partnership in his business if I could stay here permanently, but you and I both know I can't do that."

"Can't you, Charles?" Amy hated to beg, and she knew she was doing exactly that; but her heart was breaking, and she had to make one desperate try.

"Don't make this harder on me than it already is, Amy. I promised Melinda I would return to the red hills and build a home for her there. She's lost everything in the world except me, and I expect by now she's decided she's lost me too. She has no one else. I can't abandon her, Amy. I just can't."

"Then I wish you well," Amy said stiffly, trying to salvage what was left of her pride. "I wish I had something to give you to take with you. Something to remember us by."

"You have. You've given me the most precious gift in the world—one I will take with me wherever I go for the rest of my life."

Her questioning look caused him to continue. "You've shown me the way back to God, Amy. I had almost lost my way for awhile, until you showed me the path back. I won't be a backslider ever again. I'm a new man for having known you. As for remembering you. . . Dear Amy, do you really think I could ever forget you?"

Amy turned her back to him, fighting a new outpouring of

tears. "I'd better get back to the shop. I promised the girls I'd be there to lock up."

"I'll walk back with you," he said.

It was a solemn walk back to the millinery shop. She ignored his proffered arm, quickening her step. Part of Amy wanted to hold on to him, to never let him go; and another part of her wanted to run as fast as she could, back to the solitude of her room where she could cry her heart out without being heard.

# twenty-two

July and August dragged by with scarcely any rain. Dust from the streets poured into the open windows of Amy's upstairs room, yet she had to leave them open to coax the gulf breeze through in an attempt to break the stifling heat.

Business in the shop had diminished to almost nothing. It was simply too hot for the ladies to don their long dresses and layers of petticoats to do unnecessary shopping; and with yellow fever continuing its rampage, people were reluctant to mingle in crowded places. Just last week Amy had seen two new yellow flags hanging as ominous reminders that the terrible disease was still a threat, and news from neighboring Saint Joe was even more devastating.

Because well-bred ladies stayed out of sight during the final weeks of confinement, Margaret didn't come into the shop to help at all anymore. Amy found the days long without Margaret's companionship and visited her at home whenever she had the opportunity.

She didn't allow herself to admit how much she missed Charles. If she cried herself to sleep at night, she waited until after her candles were extinguished. Only then could she smother her sobs in her pillow and keep her lonely, aching heart a secret.

Alex was up early each morning to deliver his newspapers before reporting for work at the general store. He was delighted when Mr. Diamanti hired him to help stock the shelves and deliver groceries to the customers. The kind grocer had apologized over and over to Alex and to Amy too for having accused Alex of stealing his gold. Now he seemed to be trying to make it up to the boy by giving him a summer job in the general store.

Amy dressed in loose cotton shifts and only one petticoat, attempting to stay as cool as possible while she went about her daily chores. She tried to keep her outdoor activities to a minimum; but food spoiled rapidly in the midsummer heat, and a daily trip to the general store was a necessity.

The noon hour seemed to be the most convenient time to leave her shop, but some days she simply could not face the midday heat and waited until dusk to go out to make her purchases.

On this day, she waited until just before sunset. With a basket over her arm and a grocery list in her reticule, she set off down the street. By the time she reached the store, her garments were sticking to her body, and she used her handkerchief to blot the dampness from her face.

The store was crowded, giving evidence that many people waited to do their shopping when the sun went down. In spite of Mr. Diamanti's penchant for cleanliness, the indoor air reeked of sour perspiration and talcum powder. Amy pulled her list from her reticule, determined to shop quickly and return home, where she could shed some of her outer clothing.

"Hello, Mrs. McCutcheon."

At first Amy didn't recognize Mattilou with her sleek, shoulder-length hair. She seemed to have lost some weight, as well as her long, dangling curls and some of her shyness. "Why, hello, Mattilou. Are you enjoying your summer vacation?"

"Yes, Ma'am. I'm—"

Mrs. Simpson stepped in front of her daughter. "She may be enjoying it, but she's wearing me out," the lady declared. "Imagine, in this heat, she's decided she wants to learn to cook. She's tried out nearly every cookie recipe in my book and keeps insisting we come down here to the store to get more sugar, or more vanilla, or whatever her newest recipe calls for. I declare, I don't know what happens to all those cookies she bakes."

"Well, congratulations, Mattilou. I'm sure you'll turn out to be a fine cook." *Imagine that! Mrs. Simpson actually spoke to me in a near-civilized manner. Granted, she was complaining, but at least her complaints weren't directed against me.*

Amy gave Mattilou and her mother a friendly smile before she turned to the bushel basket of potatoes to select some nice ones for supper.

Amy moved to the meat counter at the back of the store and ordered two pork chops for supper. Alex always came home starved. "Some nice lean ones, please, Mr. Diamanti." The storekeeper cut two thick chops from a loin, weighed them, and wrapped them in brown paper. Amy glanced around the store, but her son was nowhere in sight. "Alex is so pleased to have a job for the summer," she said. "I hope he is proving to be helpful."

"Oh, my, yes. All the ladies want their groceries delivered these hot days. Some of them bring in their lists for the whole week, and each day Alex takes them a portion of what they've ordered. I don't know how I could manage without him." He added a meaty soup bone to her package before he secured it with a string. "He's out on a delivery now, but he should be back soon. I'll need him to take these things over to Mrs. Simpson's house. Would you like for him to drop off your things on the way?"

"Oh, no, thank you, Mr. Diamanti. I'll just carry them home in my basket." At the front counter she paid for her purchases and left. It would be only a slight bit out of her way to walk by Margaret's house, and she could put her chops in the icebox until she was ready to go home.

Margaret was sitting on the veranda, a tall glass of iced tea in her hand. "Oh, Amy! What a treat! I declare, I think I am going mad sitting here day after day with nothing to do but fan myself and complain about the heat."

Laughing, Amy climbed the front steps and gave her a hug. "I doubt that, Margaret. If I know you, you're just as busy as ever and just as sweet."

"Let's go inside and fix you a glass of iced tea. Then we can come back here and talk. At least there's always a breeze on the porch."

Amy followed her friend into the house. "Could I put my meat in your icebox until I'm ready to leave?" *What a convenience it must be to have an icebox where things stay cold for several days and one can enjoy the luxury of chipped ice in a glass of tea every day!*

"Of course." Margaret's loose gown billowed around her rounded body as she waddled toward the kitchen. She took Amy's package of meat and placed it over the ice. Then she used an ice pick to chop frozen slivers from the block and put them into a tall glass for her guest.

Sitting in white wicker rocking chairs, sipping tea so cold it numbed their teeth, the two friends watched the sun's slow westward descent as it tinted the clouds with purple and gold. "Mikal should be home soon," Margaret said. "Why don't you stay and have a light supper with us? I don't cook very much these days, but Mikal is so sweet. He never complains, even though he's working long hours since Charles left."

The reminder was like a knife in Amy's heart, but she tried not to let her face reveal her emotions. "Thanks, but I really have to get back to cook supper for Alex. He's always so hungry when he gets home. I just wanted to stop in to make sure you're still feeling well. Did you finish that carriage cover you were knitting?"

"No, but I've made six pairs of booties, all of them blue. I gave up on the carriage cover because I couldn't stand that much wool yarn in my lap. I'll make a coverlet for his carriage as soon as the weather cools down a bit. I won't be taking him out soon anyway. Not until the threat of yellow fever goes away. John says there are six new cases in town."

"Terrible," Amy agreed, rising from the rocker. "Now, you just keep your seat and watch for Mikal. I'll slip in and get my meat from your icebox and be on my way."

Margaret stood and stretched her back. "No, I'm coming in too. The mosquitoes will soon begin their nightly attack, and anyway, I can't sit in one position for long at a time." She led the way to the kitchen to retrieve the brown paper package. "Here you are, Amy. Please come again soon. You don't know how much your visits help me."

Amy placed the parcel in her basket and started toward the porch. "It helps me too, Margaret. I'll get back again soon, I promise. In the meanwhile, send for me if you need me for anything." She stopped and kissed her best friend on the cheek before she stepped outside into the evening air, already beginning to cool in the purple twilight.

❧

Amy unloaded her basket and put her groceries away. She peeled and cut up the potatoes and put them in a pan of water. When they came to a good, rolling boil, she pushed the pan to the back of the cookstove where they would simmer until they were tender.

She had just finished frying the chops in her cast-iron skillet when she heard Alex bound up the stairs. "Hey, Mama. I'm home." He dropped his burlap sack on the table and grabbed the water pail to begin his nightly chores.

"You can do that after supper, Honey. You've been working all day. You must be starved." She tried to plant a kiss on his face, but he wriggled away and started back down the stairs with his pail.

"No, Ma'am. I—I had a little snack or two this afternoon,

so I can wait 'til later to eat."

*Wonders will never cease!* Amy hoped her son wasn't coming down with something. With so much sickness in the area, any unusual behavior was immediately viewed with suspicion as a possible symptom of yellow fever. She'd feel his forehead when he came back up, just to make sure he wasn't feverish.

When she picked up his sack from the table, she was surprised to see crumbs falling from it onto her freshly scrubbed floor. She grabbed her broom and dustpan to get them up as quickly as she could. Crumbs could attract roaches and mice— or worse.

Amy examined the contents of her dustpan and sniffed. She had packed a lunch for Alex this morning, but these crumbs looked like chocolate, a luxury she could seldom afford to indulge in. She held his sack over the basin and shook it hard. More crumbs tumbled out—chocolate and yellow crumbs. Then with a thump, something else fell out. Two giant cookies showed signs of having been nibbled. *Where did they come from?* Amy wondered. She tried to imagine who might have been so generous as to supply her son with home-baked cookies.

When realization crept into her mind, Amy chuckled. *Mattilou!* She put the two unfinished cookies back into his sack and closed it. No wonder Alex wasn't so hungry tonight! Her discovery explained many things.

She didn't question Alex about the cookies, and neither did he volunteer any information; but she put aside her worry about his lagging appetite and talked to him about his work at the general store.

While Amy washed the dishes, Alex completed his chores and fell into bed. She should have sent him out back to the pump to wash up, but she didn't have the heart to disturb him. He'd get little enough sleep before it was time to wake and deliver his morning papers.

Amy dreaded the lonely nights when she could no longer push thoughts of Charles from her mind. She wondered if he had rebuilt his home yet and if Melinda was as happy at his return as he had imagined she would be. If only—but no, she must not allow herself to dream of the impossible. Instead she whispered a silent prayer for his continued safety and happiness.

She poured her dirty dishwater into a pail for Alex to empty when morning came. She would read a few chapters from her Bible and then get ready for bed.

She had barely begun to read when she heard a knock on the door—a gentle tap at first and then a pounding. "Mrs. McCutcheon. Come quick and open the door."

Who would dare to knock on her door at this hour? The male voice did not sound familiar, and she wasn't going to unlatch her door until he identified himself. She held her candle in her hand as she hurried down the stairs.

The pounding continued. "Who is it?" she called. "The shop is closed until tomorrow. What do you want?"

"Mr. Mikal Lee sent me, Ma'am. He sent his carriage to fetch you. Said for me to bring you back fast as I can. Miss Margaret, she needs help."

Amy dashed back upstairs to scribble a note to Alex and to grab her reticule. She tied a calico bonnet over her hair and ran back down the steps. "I'm coming," she assured the messenger. She stepped out onto the porch and locked the door behind her.

The driver helped her into the waiting phaeton and urged the horses to a fast trot. He hadn't explained his mission except to say that Margaret needed help. "What is this all about?" Amy asked. "Are you sure it isn't Dr. Gorrie you're supposed to pick up?"

"No, Ma'am. We tried that earlier. Dr. Gorrie is out on a sick call. We even tried to get Miss Sabrina, the midwife from over in the quarters, but she's off helping another lady. I reckon it must be the new moon that's stirring up all these babies."

Amy felt as if a flock of butterflies had taken up residence in her stomach. She was more than willing to help her friend, but what could she do? She had never helped with the delivery of a baby. "Surely there must be someone around here who knows what to do at a time like this."

The carriage pulled up in front of the Lees' house, and the driver hopped out to help Amy down. Mikal met her at the front door. "Thank God you are here, Amy."

"While you're thanking Him, you'd better ask Him to show me what to do," Amy responded. "I've never so much as helped with a delivery before."

"But you've had a child. You must know something about it," Mikal insisted. He led her into the bedroom where Margaret lay moaning on the bed.

Amy hurried to her side. "Bring me some cloths and cool water so I can sponge her face. And you'd better put a pan of water on the stove to boil." Amy barked orders like she'd done this a thousand times before. "Find me some scissors and string and all the clean sheets you can get your hands on, and then go out and leave us alone. I think we have a long night ahead of us. You might still try to find that midwife and bring her here if you can."

When Mikal left to follow her commands, Amy bent over Margaret and said with all the assurance she could muster, "Everything is going to be fine, Margaret. Soon all the pain will be over, and you will have a beautiful baby."

❧

Dawn streaked the eastern sky with gold when Amy finally opened the bedroom door and came out carrying a tiny bundle wrapped in a square of blue flannel. Tiny fists poked through the opening and pummeled the air.

"How is my wife?" Mikal asked, vaulting toward the door.

His eyes were bloodshot, and his blond hair straggled down across his forehead. "Is Margaret all right? Can I see her now?"

"Margaret is fine," Amy assured him. "Just tired, that's all. And of course you can see her, but don't you want to see your baby first?"

"Is he—?"

"No, Mikal. *He* isn't anything. Let me introduce you to your new baby daughter." She thrust the bundle into his arms, and Mikal looked down in astonishment.

"My. . .my. . .did you say 'daughter'?" He held the baby as if she were a piece of fine crystal.

Amy laughed, pushing stray tendrils of dark hair from her damp face. "Yes, Mikal. You are the father of a beautiful, healthy baby girl. Now take her in to her mother, and the three of you can thank God for the blessing He has bestowed on you this day."

When Mikal went into the bedroom carrying his precious bundle, Amy closed the door behind him. This would be a special time for the parents to get acquainted with the newest member of their family. They didn't need anyone else.

Amy picked up her reticule and started home.

## twenty-three

Amy waited two days before calling on Margaret to hold the precious baby she herself had delivered. *"I can do all things through Christ which strengtheneth me."* Those were the words that had sustained her throughout the amazing birth of Margaret's baby.

If anyone had told her she would even assist at such an event, she would have scoffed at the idea. But from the moment she had entered Margaret's bedroom, she had felt God's hands on her own, guiding her along each step of the way.

She used the brass knocker on the front door to announce her presence, and Mikal himself opened it to welcome her. From deep inside the house, Amy heard the demanding cries of a newborn infant. She smiled. "I see there is nothing wrong with her lungs."

"Nothing wrong with anything about her," Mikal agreed. "She's the most beautiful baby I've ever seen. Perfect in every way."

"Almost as good as a boy?" Amy chided and watched as his temper momentarily flared.

"Are you implying that I'd have preferred a son?" he asked. "I'd hoped for a girl all along, but I never voiced it because I didn't want to seem disappointed if we had a boy."

Amy couldn't restrain an outburst of laughter. "Of course you did, Mikal. Now show me this child prodigy I helped into the world."

Mikal laughed too. "Margaret will be delighted you're here. She's been asking for you." He led her into the bedroom where Margaret, pretty in a pink satin bed jacket, lay propped up on pillows, cuddling her baby daughter to her breast. The cries had been replaced by a soft, smacking sound.

"Amy!" Margaret's sudden elation disturbed the baby, who protested with a yelp of indignation before settling back down to the comfort and sedation of her mother's milk.

Mikal stood in the doorway, grinning. "John Gorrie came by right after you left, Amy. He said you did a marvelous job. I think he plans to ask you to become his birthing assistant."

"I can assure you that will never happen," Amy vowed. She bent over the infant to get a closer look. "She's beautiful."

Margaret pulled back the blue flannelette blanket to expose ten tiny red toes. "Look, Amy. Isn't she just perfect?"

"What have you named her?"

Mikal and Margaret exchanged conspiratorial glances. "You tell her, Mikal."

"We've named her America after you, our dearest friend."

"Oh, my!" Amy's eyes glistened with emotion. "Such a big name for such a little girl."

"I imagine that's what they said about you when your name was chosen. But we've worked that all out," Margaret said. "Since you've chosen to be called 'Amy,' we've decided to call our little girl 'Merry.' America Lee. It has a nice ring, doesn't it?"

Amy blinked back her tears. "I don't know what to say. This is the biggest compliment I've ever been given. When do I get to hold my namesake? Is she done eating yet?"

Little America had fallen asleep at her mother's breast. "She eats all the time," Margaret said. "At this rate, she'll be as fat as a pig." She pulled her daughter away gently and straightened her blanket. "Here, Amy. Put her over your shoulder and pat her back. See if you can get a bubble."

Amy cuddled the child and patted her softly, crooning a prayer in her ear. "Darling little Merry, may you grow in God's grace, and may He grant you all His blessings. You are surrounded by love, little one."

America responded with a hearty burp, and Amy returned her to her mother. "I have to go now. It's past time to open the shop, but I couldn't wait a minute longer to see this special child again and to make sure you didn't need my help for anything."

"Do come again soon, Amy. I won't be going out much for awhile; but when I do, you can be sure my first visit will be to the millinery shop."

"Thank you so much for everything, Amy," Mikal said, placing his arm around her shoulders. "I hope little Merry grows up to be as kind and as generous as the woman whose name she shares. When she's older, she'll be told how you guided her into this world."

Amy took one more peek at the sleeping infant before she blew Margaret a kiss and scooted out the door.

❧

August afternoons seemed to drag by in the millinery shop. During the busy season, Amy often wished for afternoons like these; but now she realized how much she appreciated her customers, even on the days when she didn't have time to stop for her own needs.

She was seated at a table sewing fine pin tucks in the bodice of a blue batiste gown when she heard footsteps on the porch. She folded her work and stood up when the bell over the door jingled.

"Can I help you?" she asked, then gasped. She hadn't recognized him at first. In his gentleman's attire, he looked nothing like the stranger who had come looking for work almost a year ago; but when he smiled, there was no mistaking that dear face that invaded her dreams each night. "Charles!"

Clinging to his arm was a beautiful young girl. Tall and willowy, her blond curls fell loosely about her shoulders. Her shy smile marked her unmistakably as Charles's sister. "You must be Melinda."

"Yes. And you are Amy."

Charles, his eyes unwavering, seemed to drink in the sight of her. At last he spoke. "Amy, I've missed you so. I've counted the days until I could return."

"I–I wasn't sure you planned to return," she told him. "A great deal has happened since you've been away." Her heart had been broken when he left. Would he leave again? She wasn't going to open herself to that kind of pain again. Why had he returned?

"Hey, Mama. I'm—" Alex stopped short in his tracks when he saw they had visitors. Like Amy, he took a few minutes to realize who they were. "Mr. Drake? And—" He raised questioning eyes at the pretty girl in the bright yellow gown.

"This is my sister, Melinda," Charles explained. "Melinda, this is Amy's son, Alex." The young people exchanged shy smiles, and Charles offered a suggestion. "Alex, I've been telling my sister about the wonderful smoked oysters they sell on the waterfront. Do you suppose you could take her down there to try them?" He reached into his pocket and pulled out a handful of coins. "My treat, of course."

"Why, sure," Alex said, pocketing the coins. "Come on, Melinda. Maybe we can walk out on the pier and look for porpoises. Ever seen a porpoise?"

"No, but I'd like to," she said, following Alex to the front door.

"Alex, stop by the pump and wash your face and hands, Honey."

"Aw, Mama."

Charles chuckled. "Let them be, Amy. Alex is almost a man, and he's fine just the way he is." Alex cast him a smile of appreciation before he led Melinda to the porch.

"Alone with you at last," Charles said, covering the space between them in two easy strides and pulling her into his arms. But Amy, using all her willpower, pushed him away.

"Would you like a cup of tea?" She tried to keep her voice from quavering.

Charles heaved an exasperated sigh. "No, I *do not* want tea. What's wrong, Amy? Don't you have any feelings for me anymore?"

"I'm very happy to see you, Charles. Of course I have feelings for you. You're a. . .a very dear friend." Somehow this was all coming out wrong. She longed to be in his arms, to hear him say he loved her; but he had never told her that, and until he did, she mustn't bare her heart.

"A friend? Is that all I am to you, Amy? Somehow I thought we had more than that. I want you to know that I've been miserable without you. I thought I could start over again and build a life without you. I tried, but I just can't do it."

"This is all moving too fast, Charles. As I told you, much has happened since you've been gone."

Blood drained from his face, and he looked as though he had received a severe blow. "What are you saying? Have you found someone else?"

Amy turned her back to him. She couldn't conceal her feelings as long as she looked into those penetrating blue eyes. "You've been gone a very long time, Charles, and I've heard nothing from you. Tell me what you've been doing since you left."

"You know how unreliable the mails are. I had to wait until I could come to you in person. To be honest, I didn't know what I should do. I only knew I had to build my future with you. Please turn around and look at me."

Amy sank into a chair, and Charles pulled one alongside. Without meeting his direct gaze, she said, "Melinda is a lovely girl. Have you built a house for her yet?"

Charles reached for her hands. "No, I haven't. After we talked about it, Melinda decided she'd like to begin a new life in a new place without so many painful memories. I've told her about Apalachicola, and she thought she might learn to be happy here."

In spite of the warning bells clanging in her head, Amy's

heart soared with hope. "But what about your land in the red hills? And. . .and all your livestock?"

"Melinda and I made the decision together to sell our land to the Marchmans. These are the kind people who took care of Melinda after the fire. They own the acreage adjacent to ours. I'll never be able to repay them for the loving way they cared for my sister while I was away, so I was glad we were able to offer them a very fair price for our land and all the livestock. They can't pay in cash, but I know they'll pay in full whenever they can. I trust them completely, and the extra land and animals will boost their family income by a substantial amount. Dan Marchman expects to be debt free in three years."

He drew her to her feet and tried again to embrace her. "Amy, I love you so."

This time when he held her close, she did not draw away but instead reached up to encircle his neck with her slender arms and draw his face down near her level. "Do you mean that, Charles? Because you've never said that to me before."

"That I love you? Of course—I mean it with all my heart. I've wanted to tell you so many times before, but I never felt I had the right until now. I'm asking you to be my wife; and if you say yes, we will work together to make a home for Alex and Melinda with Christ as its cornerstone. Will you marry me, Amy?"

Amy gasped and struggled to catch her breath. "I've waited so long to hear you say those words. Yes, I'll marry you, my darling. With God's help, I'll be the kind of wife you deserve and a worthy substitute for the mother Melinda loved and lost."

He gathered her in his arms, and his lips claimed hers in a kiss that was at once tender and passionate. Amy felt the thrill of it like a vibrant shock that began at her toes and traveled all the way up to the top of her head, leaving her reeling and breathless.

"You've made me the happiest man in the world," he said before he kissed her again. "Let's go find the children and tell them the good news."

# epilogue

On November 15, in a simple ceremony in Apalachicola's beautiful Trinity Church, America McCutcheon became the bride of Charles Drake.

Amy, with a bit of help from Priscilla and Rachel, had made her own wedding dress from a piece of palest blue silk. Elegant in its simplicity, the gown featured tiny covered buttons down the back of the tightly fitted, V-pointed bodice and again on the long pointed sleeves. Margaret fashioned the bride's head-piece of delicate silk flowers entwined with lustrous pearls.

Alex escorted Melinda to their special place of honor in the beribboned front pew. Then, as the church musician pumped wedding music from the organ, Margaret walked down the aisle to serve as Amy's only attendant, and Mikal led the glowing bride down to the altar to meet her waiting groom.

After the ceremony, the wedding party and friends gathered for a gala reception at the home of Mikal and Margaret Lee. A large, flower-bedecked wedding cake was the focal point of the lace-covered dining table. After they shared the first piece, Amy and Charles cut the cake into slices and shared them with their guests.

Amy smiled as she watched her son. When had he grown so tall? Trying to live up to his grown-up role, he brought Melinda a cup of punch to go with her cake. "I reckon you're almost like my sister now," Amy heard him tell her.

"I reckon so," she agreed. "Do you mind terribly?"

Alex shrugged his shoulders. "Not if you don't."

"Isn't it time to throw the bouquet?" Priscilla asked eagerly.

"I suppose it is," Amy agreed. She had never been happier. "Line up over there, and I'll toss it over my shoulder."

Priscilla and Rachel pushed to the front of the small group of young women, transparent in their desires to be the lucky recipient.

"All right now, get ready! One, two, three!" The bouquet of pink rosebuds sailed through the air and landed right in the hands of Melinda, who stood shyly off to one side. The squealing group of hopefuls with their hands in the air gave a collective sigh of disappointment.

Melinda gasped with delight. "For me? I get to keep it?"

"Indeed you do," Amy assured her. She gave the girl a hug. "I have to go change clothes now, Melinda, but Charles and I will see you again before we leave."

Charles appeared to have a hard time trying to keep up with his new bride. Everyone seemed to be vying for her attention. Now it was Margaret who whisked her away. "Time to change clothes," she said, grabbing Amy's arm and pulling her toward the bedroom.

Margaret allowed no one else in the bedroom while Amy changed into her traveling outfit. This would be their last chance for real girl talk until the newlyweds returned from their wedding trip to New Orleans.

Amy slipped her new gabardine dress over her head, and Margaret began the tedious task of fastening the buttons down the back.

"Are you sure having Alex and Melinda stay with you isn't going to be too much trouble, Margaret?" Amy asked.

"Don't be silly, Amy. Melinda is such a help with Merry. And you know how much Mikal enjoys Alex. He makes up for that son Mikal didn't get." Both women laughed, remembering how Mikal had carried on about having a son before Merry was born.

"Well, maybe your next one will be a boy," Amy teased, and Margaret slapped her playfully on the arm.

"I expect the next one to be yours, Amy." When Amy widened her eyes in shock, Margaret reminded her, "You aren't even thirty yet. There's still plenty of time for you and Charles to enlarge your family."

"Margaret, this is hardly the time to be talking to me like this. I'm nervous enough as it is."

"Hold still," Margaret commanded. "I have six more buttons to fasten. I didn't mean to make you nervous. I just couldn't help but wonder why Charles is building your new house with so many bedrooms. Maybe he plans for you to take in boarders." She laughed, and Amy swung around and put her hands in the air, ready to give her friend a scolding. Instead they both burst into a fit of laughter that ended in a warm hug.

"We'd better hurry," Margaret reminded her. "You're due at the dock in an hour, and those steamboats don't wait."

A knock sounded on the door. "Is my bride ready to go?"

Amy was too nervous to answer, so Margaret answered for her. "She's ready, Charles. You may come in and get her."

When Amy saw her new husband enter the room, all her anxiety melted like butter on a warm day, and she hurried to meet him.

They raced out of the house, through the crowd of people, amid showers of rice, and soon reached the waiting carriage. "Just a moment, Charles. We have one more thing to do. Where are Alex and Melinda?"

"We're here," the two children called, pushing their way through the crowd of people.

Amy and Charles hugged first one and then the other before telling them good-bye. "Our children!" she said proudly. "In a few days we'll be back from our wedding trip, and maybe by Christmas, our new home will ready for us to move into. Then we'll feel like a real family." As the carriage rolled down the street, Amy leaned out and waved for as long as she could see them. Then she turned to her new husband and leaned into his arms.

God was so good. She only needed to trust Him. He always worked everything out for good in His time.

# Historical Notes

The yellow fever epidemic of 1841, coupled with a devastating hurricane in 1844, literally destroyed Apalachicola's rival cotton port of Saint Joseph.

Because of the prevalence of yellow fever during the hot summer months, especially in tropical climates, Dr. John Gorrie was convinced that his "cooling machine" could reduce or prevent the dreaded disease. It was not until 1901 that mosquitoes were named as the carrier of the yellow fever virus and of malaria as well.

John Gorrie received a patent on his ice machine in 1848. He is credited with the invention of the first ice machines and is recognized as a pioneer in refrigeration and air-conditioning. But because of problems in product demand and operation, along with the opposition of the ice lobby, he never realized any return from his invention. He is buried in Apalachicola in Gorrie Square, where a museum features memorabilia, including a replica of his first ice machine. The original machine is displayed in the Smithsonian Institute in Washington, D.C.

Trinity Church is on the National Register of Historic Places and is open to visitors. Regular worship services are still held there.

The lock-stitch sewing machines from which modern machines descended did not appear until later in the century, and the chain-stitch machine the Lees obtained in New York in 1840 was a rarity generally available only for commercial operations.

Florida achieved statehood in 1845 and ceased to provide a haven for rustlers and outlaws. Today the territory once known as the red hills is a serene and beautiful area of northwest Florida.

A visit to the quaint little town of Apalachicola, Florida, where people still boast of the best oysters in the world, promises to be enjoyable, enlightening, and not easily forgotten.

# A Letter To Our Readers

Dear Reader:

In order that we might better contribute to your reading enjoyment, we would appreciate your taking a few minutes to respond to the following questions. We welcome your comments and read each form and letter we receive. When completed, please return to the following:

Fiction Editor
Heartsong Presents
PO Box 719
Uhrichsville, Ohio 44683

1. Did you enjoy reading *Red Hills Stranger* by Muncy G. Chapman?
   ❑ Very much! I would like to see more books by this author!
   ❑ Moderately. I would have enjoyed it more if

   _____

   _____

   _____

2. Are you a member of **Heartsong Presents**? ❑ Yes ❑ No
   If no, where did you purchase this book? _____

   _____

3. How would you rate, on a scale from 1 (poor) to 5 (superior), the cover design? _____

4. On a scale from 1 (poor) to 10 (superior), please rate the following elements.

   ____ Heroine          ____ Plot
   ____ Hero             ____ Inspirational theme
   ____ Setting          ____ Secondary characters

5. These characters were special because?_____

_____

_____

6. How has this book inspired your life?_____

_____

_____

7. What settings would you like to see covered in future
   **Heartsong Presents** books? _____

_____

_____

8. What are some inspirational themes you would like to see
   treated in future books? _____

_____

_____

9. Would you be interested in reading other **Heartsong
   Presents** titles?  ❑ Yes  ❑ No

10.  Please check your age range:
    ❑ Under 18            ❑ 18-24
    ❑ 25-34               ❑ 35-45
    ❑ 46-55               ❑ Over 55

Name_____

Occupation _____

Address _____

City_____ State_____ Zip_____

Email_____

# Gold Rush Christmas

*W*hen the "Gold Fever" epidemic sweeps the nation in 1849, people drop everything to chase the dream of striking it rich. Follow one family's itch for adventure from California to the Rockies to Alaska—and discover a Christmas gift more valuable than gold.

Four Christmases in gold country prove life's most priceless gifts come not in the form of polished gold—but from the vast riches of a loving heart.

Historical, paperback, 352 pages, 5 $\frac{3}{16}$"x 8 "

❤ ❤ ❤ ❤ ❤ ❤ ❤ ❤ ❤ ❤ ❤ ❤ ❤ ❤ ❤ ❤ ❤ ❤ ❤

Please send me ____ copies of *Gold Rush Christmas* I am enclosing **$6.99** for each. (Please add **$2.00** to cover postage and handling per order. OH add 7% tax.)

**Send check or money order, no cash or C.O.D.s please.**

Name _____

Address _____

City, State, Zip _____

**To place a credit card order, call 1-800-847-8270.**

Send to: Heartsong Presents Reader Service, PO Box 721, Uhrichsville, OH  44683

❤ ❤ ❤ ❤ ❤ ❤ ❤ ❤ ❤ ❤ ❤ ❤ ❤ ❤ ❤ ❤ ❤ ❤ ❤

# Presents

## Great Inspirational Romance at a Great Price!

Heartsong Presents books are inspirational romances in contemporary and historical settings, designed to give you an enjoyable, spirit-lifting reading experience. You can choose wonderfully written titles from some of today's best authors like Peggy Darty, Sally Laity, Tracie Peterson, Colleen L. Reece, Debra White Smith, and many others.

*When ordering quantities less than twelve, above titles are $3.25 each.*
*Not all titles may be available at time of order.*